WHO HOLDS THE HANDS
of Thyme

WHO HOLDS THE HANDS
of Thyme

A Novel of the Old South

Margaret Joanne Rice

J. Kenkade
PUBLISHING®
LITTLE ROCK, ARKANSAS

Who Holds the Hands of Thyme
Copyright © 2019 by Margaret Joanne Rice

J. Kenkade Publishing
6104 Forbing Rd
Little Rock, AR 72209
www.jkenkadepublishing.com
Facebook.com/jkenkadepublishing

J. Kenkade Publishing is a registered trademark.

Printed in the United States of America
ISBN 978-1-944486-93-8

Contents

INTRODUCTION

Life in the Southern United States pre- and post-Civil War was a civilization of its own. You could say society in the South was basically made of two groups of people: "the haves" and "the have-nots". The elite plantation owners had much money, influence, and power. They owned many acres of land. They had many possessions, including workers on the farms.

This story takes place in Staunton, Virginia, and centers on the lives of several people on that plantation. Cadelia, a black cook in the big house, is a motivating person. She is wise and respected by her fellow workers and the plantation owners. This story, though, deals with another civilization that we tend to forget. The Native Americans are a central part of this story. So many times, we forget that they were the original inhabitants of the United States.

White Feather, a well-respected Shawnee Indian businessman, owns a trading post on one side of town. The Negroes are very superstitious people, and they have numerous encounters with the Indian ancestral spirits. Many times, the only way problems can be solved is by having White Feather contact his spiritual ancestors on the matter. Upon a series of unexplainable and supernatural events, Miss Cadelia and the black workers seek White Feather's advice to solve their problems.

Ancient Native American customs and beliefs are very sacred. The red man was very much aware that the white people had exploited and literally confiscated and stolen all their property and land. The American government called it a legal and legitimate takeover: in exchange for their lands, the American government had allotted lands out in the West where the Indians lived. These were called reservations.

The Shawnee Indians were given a vision, influenced by a message sent by their ancestors, that one day a child would be born, and this child would have extraordinary spirits, insights and visions. He would be able to retrieve all the property that was stolen by the white man. The Indians had to be patient and await the birth of this special child.

The story centers on a very prestigious family, The Stauntons. The family patriarch is Carlton Staunton. His brother is Dr. Theodore Staunton. Carlton believes in running a top-notch plantation. He is a fair man and treats all his workers with respect. He provides for them and feels a responsibility to all of them.

Teddy is a widowed medical doctor. He travels to all parts of the community to minister to all medical needs. Both men work closely to earn a living for the occupants of Staunton Plantation.

The children in this family are raised in a very elite lifestyle. They are sent to the best boarding schools to get a proper education. In these schools, they meet their future mates, who are elite in their own hometowns. Many interesting escapades take place at Wilshire Academy, a women's boarding school.

There are floods, cattle drives, and plagues to be dealt with. Many of the old Indian beliefs come to life in this story, and problems are only solved by the wise council of

White Feather. The exciting flood in this story is a perfect example. The old grandfather clock on the bottom floor of the Staunton mansion is a central symbol in this story. Many strange Indian mysteries are locked in this clock. The whole plantation and the lives of its workers are at risk. The old grandfather clock is of great significance, as it literally holds the "Hands of Time". The clock knows the exact date, year, time and hour that the Native American Savior will be born, and the American Indians anxiously await the baby's arrival.

CHAPTER 1

Meet the Stauntons

His name is Cotton. He is a Negro blacksmith on Dad's plantation, and he is spooky. I love to hide in the stables and listen to the stories he tells. If he has a responsive audience, and he usually does, the stories will go on for hours and hours. I don't know if the stories are true or not, but the Negroes at Staunton Plantation swear by every word he says.

Aunt Martha is coming next week. Dad says the tobacco business will take him out of town quite a bit, and he hates to leave me for long periods of time.

Miss Cadelia is a grand person. She is a marvelous cook, but she is not good at calculus or physics. The schools out east require much mathematics and science. Aunt Martha is a retired mathematics teacher, so Dad figured she would be perfect for the job. Uncle Josh will remain in San Bernardino, California while Aunt Martha spends most of the summer with me – tutoring long hours, I'm sure.

Dad says the tobacco industry is faring well, and Virginia is the place to be. Calcutta is my best friend. I wish I could pack him up in my traveling bag when I go to finishing school. I know I'll miss him a lot.

Each Sunday we have a Sunday dinner at Staunton Plantation. My Uncle Teddy and his children always eat with us. My Uncle Teddy is the local doctor. After eating, the grown-ups shove us kids out the front door, while they discuss all the family matters. Teddy and Dad are business partners. Dad does the groundwork, and Uncle Teddy sells to our Eastern customers. Anyway, both men run the family business, selling tobacco products and Appaloosa ponies. They are out of town quite a lot, traveling from Staunton to Washington, D.C. and the Middle Eastern states. Therefore, Uncle Teddy and his children are with us quite a lot. I don't mind Cousin George or Cousin Sabrina, but prissy Miss Agnes I could do without. Oh, yeah, she has a trail of boyfriends (one for every day of the week), but she calls me her best friend, and I get sick just thinking about her.

George is ten, and he is a chicken little. He is scared of his own shadow. When we are together, I'm always the boss. He is not very dependable, if you know what I mean.

Sabrina is just plain fun. She can outrun a rabbit and outride any boy in Virginia. She is loads of fun, if you can catch her. That's enough of the ramifications; it's time to get on with the story.

"There's no way you can do all that," said Jessica.

"I swear, Jess," George replied. "I swear on the Bible."

"You are crazy," she answered. "I do not believe a word you say."

Sabrina jumped off the steps and pushed George back toward the old fence post.

"Show us, then – right now!" she demanded. "Show us!"

George picked up the rifle, and all three of them headed out toward the pasture behind the barn. Back in the main house, another conversation was going on.

"Carlton, now just who is this woman?" asked Teddy.

"She's just an auditor," Carlton responded. "The state auditor with Central Guarantee Bank. She is going to be with us a few days. Something about annexing the property."

Then Teddy asked, "Has the paperwork been cleared?"

"Most of it, but she has a few more details to clear up before the final papers are drawn up."

"And how did we come about using her? You know, I am skeptical about using a woman."

"Mister Milner assured me that she is very reputable; in fact, she is the best in the State of Virginia."

"When will she arrive?"

Carlton answered, "The latter part of the summer. I do want to get this matter taken care of as soon as possible."

Teddy began to stand up from the table. Carlton stood up, also.

Then Teddy said, "Tell Miss Cadelia that we enjoyed the dinner, as always. I'm going to round the kids up, and we're going back into town. The dinner was delicious."

"I must agree it was the best! You know those chicken and dumplings are my favorite."

"Thanks, Mister Teddy," Cadelia responded.

As he took the coat and umbrella, Teddy said, "Thanks again," then continued, "I've got to be in Minter City this morning. Mrs. Ludlow is having a baby. I will probably have to take the baby. Seems like she's been having complications with this pregnancy."

"Do you anticipate any problems?" Carlton asked.

"Probably, more than we can handle."

Miss Cadelia stuck her head out the kitchen door and said, "Mister Teddy, don't forget your coat. I heard you were about to leave." Then she walked through the main hall to the coat rack. She got the coat and Mister Teddy's umbrella and handed them to him.

"You know," Miss Cadelia interjected, "I just love cooking for you boys."

Then Teddy gave Miss Cadelia a hug and a kiss on the cheek and whispered in her ear, "I love you."

CHAPTER 2

Risky-Whiskey Business

Early the next morning, shortly after daybreak, the blacksmith shop was busy with activity. The blacksmith shop was located about a fourth of a mile from the main house, on a winding dirt road. There were three men conversing with each other. Cotton was one of the Negroes who worked for Mister Staunton. Cotton had white hair. He was in his 40's, and Mister Staunton has depended on Cotton for a long time. Cotton ran the blacksmith shop, and he was very important around the plantation. He was in charge of the tobacco crop each year. The other two Negroes were not employees of Mister Staunton. One of the Negroes was kneeling on the ground drawing in the dirt, and the other was looking at the drawing, trying to understand the written message. He was also observing closely to be sure nobody else was watching them discuss this information.

Cotton spoke up. "It is a matter of safety. Safety always has to come first."

The Negro kneeling on the ground responded, "No worry, no worry, the route is safe. Folks been running these here routes since Old Man Turner blew up the Bruckner Bridge, and that was nearly two years ago."

Cotton asked, "And what about the governor?"

The second man turned to Cotton and said, "He's in favor."

"How do you know he is?" Cotton asked.

Then the Negro drawing on the ground quickly added, "Last town meeting, the spokesman from Calhoun City cornered him and got his approval; that is, as long as he got his share of the money. The governor promised to keep it quiet and legal, so I take the man at his word."

Then Cotton put his hands in his pocket, stirred his feet around on the ground and said, "What's it going to cost me?"

The Negro doing the drawing stood up and said, "I can cut you in on halves, if you are willing to run the wagons."

Cotton grinned from ear to ear. "Need you say more? I'm in."

The men shook hands with Cotton and walked off.

Early the next morning, Jessica Leigh and Miss Cadelia were in the kitchen.

"Now, Miss Jessie, you didn't eat any of your breakfast!" Miss Cadelia snapped.

"Just wasn't hungry," Jessica muttered.

"You know your father does not like you to leave this house without your breakfast," she responded. Miss Cadelia took Jessica by the shoulder and sat her back down in the kitchen chair.

"Here, at least eat your biscuit and orange marmalade."

Jessica sat back down, gobbled up the biscuit, and drank her milk.

Then Jessica got up and explained, "I gotta go, Miss Cadelia. Me and Calcutta are going to do some work on the treehouse. We are making a hideout. I gotta get started before father expects me to do my chores. If he asks, tell him I'm not up yet. I'll be back by 10 o'clock."

And before Miss Cadelia could say another word, Jessica Leigh was running out of the back door hollering for her best friend.

"Come on, boy, come on!"

The two of them were headed straight for the blacksmith shop.

As Jessica Leigh and Calcutta ran toward the blacksmith shop, Jessica Leigh talked to Calcutta.

"Calcutta," she said. "You've got to be quiet – you must be very quiet. You don't want anybody to hear us."

Calcutta began to bark, and Jessica Leigh reprimanded him again. "Sh-sh-sh."

As they got closer to the blacksmith shop, there was a little fence with a wood railing. She found a little corner on one side of the fence, and it was well within hearing distance of the blacksmith shop.

Jessica whispered, "Sh-sh, Calcutta. If they see us, they will stop talking."

Both of them sat very quietly in the little, comfortable spot next to the fence.

Miss Josie Longmire and Miss Tabatha Wrongfellow were chatting with Mister Cotton.

Apparently, the matter was quite secret because as Cotton talked he would look all around to be sure nobody was listening. Cotton did not want anyone to sneak up and hear any of the details that he was giving out.

Miss Josie was a light-colored Negro. She was probably in her late thirties. She was very thin and looked pretty tall, especially when compared to Miss Tabatha. Miss Tabatha was short and seemed very roly-poly. Both ladies were enjoying spending time with Mister Cotton.

Miss Josie whispered, "You don't say."

"My, oh my," Miss Tabatha chimed in.

"Mister Cotton," Miss Josie stated firmly. "This does sound dangerous. Are you sure it is worth the risk?"

Cotton began to explain. "Staunton Plantation will be at no risk. The stills are south of here, located in an area called Gun Point. There are three running stills and one underway. The site is so hidden, you can't make it in or out unless you have a roadmap."

"When is your first run?" Miss Tabatha asked.

Cotton replied, "Next Wednesday. All I have to do is supply the old cedar wagon and be at Gun Point at sundown, then transport the barrels across the state line, collect our money, and wait for the next haul."

"Sounds relatively easy," Miss Josie said.

"Cotton," Miss Tabatha asked, "Are you worried about Mr. Staunton? I know you didn't ask him about this matter."

"If the pressure gets on, quit. I can't think of an easier way to clear ten in three hours. Can you?"

Ms. Josie spoke up quickly. "Cotton, yo' main problem is yo' mouth. If you tell everybody on Staunton Plantation and everybody in Templeton, West Virginia about your money-making scheme, you'll lose your job and wind up in jail. Aberdeen Cotton, you be very careful. Hear me? Be very careful!"

The next week the family was gathered at Staunton Plantation for the regular Sunday dinner. They were all seated in the dining hall. There was a large family table. The two Staunton brothers sat on each end. Miss Cadelia first brought in the coffee, being that the family always chit-chatted across the table while the men were drinking their coffee. Once the main course was served, all talking ceased, and each person ate his Sunday dinner. The men might talk leisurely, but the children were expected to remain quiet. The very fine china was used, as well as the silver and crystal glassware.

"Well, Jessica Leigh," said Teddy. "I hear Aunt Martha will be here next weekend. I know you'll enjoy her being here."

Jessica Leigh responded, "I don't know about that! Daddy doesn't seem to understand that I can take care of myself."

Teddy inquired, "But what about calculus and physics?"

"What about it? I can always learn those subjects when I get to school."

Then Carlton spoke up. "Young lady, you have to be at the top of your class when you get to Wilshire Boarding Academy. So, you and Aunt Martha will have a lot to do before you leave."

He hesitated, then said, "That's enough talk. Cadelia is ready to serve."

Cadelia and two other black ladies brought in the Sunday dinner. As the family ate, Teddy looked at George's plate.

"George, son, please try to eat. You don't eat enough to

feed a bird."

George took another bite and nearly gagged. Sabrina ate all of her food and was asking for seconds. When Cadelia asked who wanted a piece of her lemon or coconut pie, however, all the children spoke up, even George. He did enjoy the sweets.

Carlton said, "When you children finish your dessert, run on outside. Teddy and I have some business to discuss. We'll be in the parlor."

The two men stood up and walked toward the parlor.

Carlton then said to Cadelia, "Bring our dessert and coffee into the parlor. We'll finish up in there."

When Cadelia returned, she brought the children their desserts. They were smiling all over. Miss Cadelia was such a good cook, and her desserts were so delicious. The children began talking and laughing since the adults were out of the room. Then Miss Cadelia came in again.

"Children, hurry up and skedaddle. I got to finish up those dishes."

George looked up with pleading eyes. "Miss Cadelia, can you slip me just a tiny little piece of pie? I won't tell."

"Got it right here for you, my pet," Miss Cadelia whispered, and she snuck him an extra piece of pie wrapped in a napkin. "Now skedaddle."

The children jumped up and ran outside. The children ran out the front door and off the front porch toward Jessica Leigh, all talking at the same time. Jessica had whispered a secret to George before the meal was served, and she had promised that she would tell all the children about it right after dinner. Needless to say, all the children were relishing the suspense and excited about hearing the mysterious secret, as they were running down the dirt road.

"This better be good!" Agnes remarked. "I don't want to spend my afternoon listening to some silly tales you've made up."

George answered back, "Oh, it's a good one all right. You know Jessica Leigh knows all the ends and outs around this here place."

"Let's go to the treehouse," Jessica said. "And I'll let you all in on my secret."

The children ran down the winding dirt road until they got to the treehouse. They climbed up the ladder and sat down in the treehouse. Jessica Leigh began to tell them about the story she had heard Cotton sharing with his visitors.

Late that night in the bunkhouse, two Negroes were making their plans. The bunkhouse was near the Negro cabins. Mr. Staunton had provided two nice cabins, and the Negroes lived in them. These Negro men were quietly leaving the bunkhouse. Being late at night, it was pitch black, but these men knew just what they had intended to do. Sneaking down the dark road, they finally arrived at the blacksmith shop. These men knew how to hook up the wagon, and they quietly harnessed the old mules for the first trip to the whiskey still. That night was stormy. Thunder and lightning lit up the sky.

"We'll be safe on the route," said one man.

"Yeah," the other man remarked. "Who would ever think about getting out in weather like this?"

"Certainly not, Cotton – I'm sure he's snoring like a log."

Hooking up the wagon, the two men headed toward the whiskey still. The wind was blowing strongly. The winding road went through the back woods with heavy brush and thickets. The road was so narrow, the wagon had a time making it through.

"What's going on?" one man questioned.

"We're not moving," the other man replied. "Seems like the wheel is stuck in the tangled vines."

"Well, get out and get it fixed – here is an ax – get out and cut the roots so we can make it through. Hurry up! We gotta be back by daybreak," the boss man demanded.

Grumbling, the other man complained to himself, "He makes me do everything." The second man knew if any money was transacted, he would get very little because Roosevelt was a shyster, and he was well aware it would not be a fifty-fifty deal.

The road was about a two-mile stretch from Staunton Plantation back into the lagoons. It had winding pathways and narrow crossings with trees, brush, and heavy bent tree vines. You could hardly see thirty feet ahead as they traveled to the still.

"Hey, there they are," the other man hollered.

"Just follow this path, and we can get to the other side."

Trudging through the backside, with the rain beating down, the wagon was hardly making it through. They finally reached the distillery.

"My, my, this is a good set up," both men exclaimed.

"It sho' is," the other man added. "Let me see, I've done heered Cotton say there were three stills. All we gotta do is load the whiskey into the wagon, drive a half-mile and transport the moonshine across the state line."

"No trouble, no sweat! We just outsmarted Cotton," Roosevelt bragged to the young man. "Wouldn't you say, wouldn't you say?"

"Well, if we don't get killed, I guess so, I guess so," the young man said.

Driving the wagon to the first still, they placed a barrel near the pot still and turned on the top cap, and the moonshine flowed smoothly into the barrel. They then filled the other two barrels. Filling the barrels three-quarters full, the men were ready to depart on their journey toward the state line. The men were feeling quite proud of themselves as they followed the back path. All at once the men began to look around. They were a little startled and shocked when two white men on horseback approached them.

"Awfully bad night to be carrying that whiskey across the state line," one of the men said.

"Illegal whiskey, I'm sure," the other man added.

"Naw, sir, naw, sir. Mister Staunton, he's done given his approval, and Cotton assured us it's all safe. It's okay! It's okay," Roosevelt stammered, fumbling for words.

"We knows Mister Cotton ain't going to do nothing to harm us folks. We rightfully his kin," the young man quickly interjected.

"Well," the larger man on horseback responded. "Let me just fill some buckshot in those barrels with a couple of holes. Then let me fill your head with a couple of holes. Then we'll see what Mister Cotton does."

The driver of the wagon turned around and headed for home. Holes were in all three barrels, leaking whiskey all the way back to the Staunton Plantation.

Around daybreak the two Negro men reached Staunton Plantation. They had left three empty whiskey barrels on the trail in the back woods.

The older man said, "That was close!"

The younger man answered, "Too close. If Cotton knowed what we had done, he would string us up by the toenails. How we going to explain the missing barrels?"

"Don't worry, Helsinki," said Roosevelt. "I'll take care of everything."

"What you gonna say?" Helsinki questioned.

"Cotton did not see us take the wagon, and he sho' didn't see us return it," said Roosevelt. "When the sun comes up, I'll take the whiskey barrels and roll 'em down alongside the creek bank, throw 'em in Purple Creek and tell Cotton those hombres from Calhoun City must have discovered the whiskey stills, 'cause several barrels are missing. Good story, wouldn't you say?"

"I figured it was a long time coming," Helsinki replied. "Them same fellows been asking a lot of questions at the saloon. Seems like lots of folks around here know our business."

"Is that true?"

"Hell no! But Cotton will believe it. He's so cockeyed in love with Ms. Tabatha Wrongfellow, he'll believe anything."

"Sounds good to me. Let's sneak on back to the cabin."

As they were quietly sneaking through their back door, Leddy Gail greeted the gentlemen.

"My, my, awfully late to be prowling around, wouldn't you say? Now just tell me what you two been up to, and with whom have you two been?"

Roosevelt answered, "Nuttin', Leddy Gail, nuttin."

Then Helsinki piped in. "Can't people walk around when they can't sleep?"

"Yeah," the older man said. "No law against that!"

Leddy Gail quickly responded, "You gotta do better than that! And if you can't, I'm going to call Cotton."

The older man said, "Hush up, Leddy Gail! Hush up! Me and Helsinki, well, we in a business all our own. Sleep on it tonight, and we might just cut you in on a nice piece of the pie. How about it, Leddy Gail?"

"Well..." she said. "Against my better judgment, count me in. But I swear if your story don't sound reasonable, I'm going to go to Mister Staunton myself and spill everything I know about you two – everything I know."

Several days later, a message arrived at the house.

Rosie answered the messenger. "Yeah...no...yes, sir."

Then Rosie went to find Miss Cadelia. Miss Cadelia was in the kitchen preparing a meal. Rosie was a much younger Negro, probably sixteen or seventeen years old.

"Miss Cadelia," Rosie said. "Mr. Ted sent a message. The lady surveyor finally arrived. He also said they would be out later on today. He said to set only two extra places because none of the children would be coming. So, he and Miss Tatum will be the only two extra guests."

Miss Cadelia thanked Rosie and then told her, "Please check on the guest rooms on the second floor. Be sure there are clean linens. Miss Tatum will be staying in the room above the parlor. So be sure it is picked up and tidy. Mr. Staunton has been expecting her all week."

"Yes ma'am!" Rosie answered.

CHAPTER 3

The Skull Appears

Rosie exited and went up to the second floor to prepare the linens in the guest room. When she opened the door, to her surprise, a black child was rummaging through the chest of drawers looking for something.

"Samantha!" Rosie hollered. "What are you doing here? You're not even supposed to be on the second floor!"

"Well, Miss Rosie, don't be mad, don't be mad," Samantha said, explaining, "Jessica stole the Bowie knife, and George told me she hid it in the cedar chest in the room above the parlor."

Before Samantha could say another word, Rosie hollered back, "I don't know about that, but you best get yo'self back to the bunkhouse because when and if Mr. Staunton knowed you wuz rummaging through the second floor, he would have yo' hide. Now, git."

Rosie went to Samantha and asked, "Did you hear me girl?"

"Yeah, yeah, but you better come look at this."

As Rosie approached Samantha, she said, "You know we can get in hot water."

Then Samantha opened the little cedar chest and pointed

for Rosie to look in it. Then Rosie screamed, "Ah, ah, ah!" like she had seen a ghost.

"What is it?" Rosie hollered.

"It looks like a skull of some kind," Samantha explained. "And looks there is a piece of paper with yellow writing."

Rosie was out of breath from shock and scared to death.

Then Rosie questioned, "What does it say?"

"You knows I can't read."

"Well…" Very much frightened, all Rosie could say was, "Well, well, well! Samantha, listen to me. Take this skull, put it in the slop jar, then carry the slop jar downstairs to the old lagoon and dump the skull in the lagoon. I'll hide the note. Now do you understand me? You got to get rid of the skull!"

"Why?" Samantha questioned.

"No matter why, you just do what I say. Get rid of the skull. Throw it in the old lagoon next to the Alligator Swamp and come back to the bunkhouse, so we can figure out what to do next. Now scoot."

"Miss Tatum is on her way," Rosie said. "And I gotta get the room ready for her."

Samantha carefully picked up the skull and some paper and put it in the slop jar. She carefully closed the lid and secretly slipped out of the room to the end of the second-floor half. She went out the side door and down the stairways, carrying the chamber pot. Heading for the lagoon, she began to think to herself, Hmm.

Instead of taking the skull to the lagoon, Samantha decided to hide the skull in her panties. She hid it under the bed in the Negro cabin. Yeah, she liked that idea. The skull was very interesting, and Samantha was intrigued by an Indian skull. How exciting! She carefully slipped it into the cabin and put it under the bed. Nobody would suspect a thing.

Later that day, a horse and buggy drove up with Dr. Theodore Dwight Staunton, better known in these parts as Dr. Teddy Staunton. Uncle Teddy was educated out east and attended the best medical schools in the country. While at Harvard, he met and fell in love with Miss Priscilla Agnes Prevost, the daughter of the late Richard Alexander Prevost. Dr. Prevost was a highly recognized man in the field of Anatomy and Research. They tell us it was love at first sight; that's what my father says. Uncle Teddy was taking the chemistry class from Dr. Prevost and had to go to his home to get a class assignment. When he saw Aunt Agnes, that was all it took. Father said Uncle Teddy, from that point on, always needed a lot of outside help.

So, needless to say, he spent every weekend and holiday at 2413 Vine St., Cambridge, MA. That was Dr. Prevost's home, and, of course, Agnes was always willing to assist the young man on any extracurricular assignments (if you know what I mean). Yes, they were inseparable, Aunt Agnes and Uncle Teddy. Anyway, the two married while Uncle Teddy was in medical school, and a little baby girl, Agnes D'Lyon, was born right away. That must be why she was so mean and spoiled.

"Anyway," Jessica continued. "Oh, well, I gotta go, I hear Father calling me, and I must try to make a good impression on Miss Tatum. I need to make a good, lady-like impression."

CHAPTER 4

The Lady Surveyor Arrives

The horse and buggy were parked in front of Staunton Plantation. Uncle Teddy helped Miss Tatum out of the buggy. They both walked up the steps, and Uncle Teddy knocked on the front door. Rosie opened the front door and said, "Good evening, Dr. Staunton, please come inside. Your brother is expecting you."

As they entered the house, Dr. Staunton said, "Thank you, Rosie. Let me introduce you to Miss Tatum. Rosie, this is Miss Tatum. Miss Tatum…Rosie Clairmont. You are well aware that she will be with us for a few days."

"Glad to meet you, Miss Tatum," Rosie said. Miss Tatum just smiled.

Then Dr. Staunton said, "Please have Christago bring the luggage in and put it in the parlor."

"It's very nice to have you with us, Miss Tatum," said Rosie. "I'll see to the luggage right away, and if you need any assistance, please feel free to ask. We take pride in having house guests."

"Thank you, Rosie, and please call me Leslie Charlene. Miss Tatum always sounds so formal."

"Leslie Charlene it is. I must run; I do have a lot to do."

As Rosie was leaving the room, she said, "Dr. Staunton, your brother is in the library. He is waiting on you all."

Dr. Staunton escorted Miss Tatum into the large library. The rows and rows of books made it obvious and apparent that this was quite a knowledgeable man. One would not expect a tobacco farmer who also bought and sold Appaloosas to be of such high scholastic quality and upbringing. Needless to say, Miss Tatum was impressed and figured that her stay there at Staunton Plantation might be more enjoyable than she had anticipated. As they entered the library, she focused on the distinguished elderly man with silver gray hair. He was dressed in an expensive brown tweed suit (international cut, no doubt.) His slim body frame was quite complementary to his kind, suntanned face.

As Dr. Staunton escorted her in, Carlton turned completely around. He had been looking out the window, and now he focused on Miss Tatum. Mr. Staunton walked over and shook her hand.

"So, nice to have you with us."

Miss Tatum used a firm grip back and said, "It is so nice to be here."

"You know, young lady, you come highly recommended."

"Yes, sir, I certainly hope so."

"Central Guaranty Bank backs you up completely and says you are the best auditor in Virginia."

Then Miss Tatum asked him, "And what do you say?"

"Why not give the lady a chance? I know your father, and I think very highly of him. But I have never had dealings with a woman before, so this will be relatively new to me."

Miss Tatum questioned, "In what way?"

Before he could answer, she said, "Relative to the fact that you fear I can't do the job or relative to the fact that you believe the feminine gender is not as knowledgeable and as responsible as the masculine gender?"

Mr. Staunton seemed agitated, and he sternly gave his response. "Neither, young lady, but relative to the fact that this is a pressurized, stressful assignment, and much of Virginia will be in my hands, as this annexing of property must be properly carried out. I have state leaders and representatives just waiting for the legalization to go ahead, so, no, ma'am, young lady. There is no way I can avoid being extremely cautious and eager to see that this project is accurately carried through. No matter male or female, I have ranchers all over Virginia waiting for the results of this annexation — we are looking for perfection with as little friction and controversy as possible."

Then Mr. Staunton looked her straight in the eyes.

"Can you handle a man's job?"

Miss Tatum answered back, "Consider it done, Mr. Staunton, consider it done."

Then she turned around and said, "I'll see myself out, and I'll see you gentlemen bright and early, let's say around four-ish in the morning."

"Goodnight, gentlemen."

Miss Tatum went up to her second-floor guest room. The two brothers were left standing together, talking to each other.

Dr. Staunton said, "Miss Cadelia has prepared a good dinner; why don't we enjoy it? Obviously, Miss Tatum is very tired."

The two men exited together to the dining room.

That night the Negro cabins were buzzing with activity. Everyone was excited with the arrival of Miss Tatum. Any time any activity happened at Staunton, all the residents of the plantation were involved. Everybody loved the excitement an outsider brought. The men were in the kitchen sitting around the old wooden table. Leddy Gail, the older black lady, was the cook – and a good cook she was. She was standing over the stove, making the last preparations.

"Samantha, Samantha," Rosie hollered all at once. "Just pray tell, what is under my bed?"

Quickly Samantha ran to Rosie and tried to quiet her down.

"Shh! Well, you are right, I wasn't even supposed to be on the second floor, much less messing around in the drawers. But, uh, but, uh—"

And before she could give her explanation, Leddy Gail was calling. "Supper's ready! Y'all come wash up. The chitlins are steaming hot and mighty delicious."

As the group was seated around the table, Rosie spoke up.

"Cotton, how long you been here on this plantation?"

Cotton began to calculate in his head, and then he began to use his fingers to get the right number.

"Well, yellow fever broke out in 1853. I was just a boy working at Clairmont Plantation in the Mississippi Delta. The fever killed off most all of us'ez. But a few slaves wuz sold to Mr. Carlton's grandfather, Clarence Goldwater Staunton. Then in 1868, we wuz all freed and given the opportunity to go northeast and live or stay and work for daily pay."

Samantha spoke up. "And of course you chose to stay

on, didn't you, Uncle Cotton?"

Then Cotton responded, "Well, not exactly. About this here same time, a young politician named Conrad Taylor pretty well convinced us coloreds that the golden opportunity lied in Cherokee, North Carolina. The Cherokee Indians had laid claim to a coal mine, and the talk was that every family around these here parts wuz uh striking it rich. All we had to do was sign up, and the landowners would provide a place to live with meals. We would be working in the coal mines, and we would give the boss a certain percentage. It sounded great; we wuz gonna be free men with a regular income."

Then Rosie asked, "Well, what happened?"

An old man in a wheelchair named Tommy Toes piped in. "Let me tell you the rest of the story. Old man Clarence Staunton was very skeptical about this arrangement from the very beginning. But you know Cotton just insisted that we check it all out. Mr. Staunton paid all expenses, and me and him and old Mose Loterhos made the trip to Cherokee, North Carolina to get all the details before we packed up all our duds to go."

Samantha blurted out, "So, what happened?"

"When we got there, the living quarters wuz filthy," Tommy Toes explained. "And the Indians swore to us we would be making a big mistake if we decided to come. They said they had not been paid in over two months. Promises, promises is all they got."

Then Cotton continued the story. "We stayed three days, and that was enough. We all knew Staunton Plantation, even as a slave, was far better than that situation. So, the three of us packed our bags and went back to Templeton, and we been here ever since."

Then Rosie questioned again, "Did any Indians ever live in these parts?"

"I'm sure they did at some time or another. Native Americans roamed all over these parts before white men settled," Cotton answered.

Then Samantha asked, "Well, do you think any Indians were ever buried in these parts?"

Tommy Toes spoke up. "Not to my recollection." And then he questioned, "Why, young lady, why do you ask?"

"Samantha," Rosie said. "Go on and tell him."

Samantha walked out to Rosie's bed, and as she was walking back to the kitchen area, she said, "I was rummaging around on the second floor, and I found this."

She held the baby Indian skull so all could see. When Leddy Gail saw the skull, she screamed really loudly and said to herself, "Not again!" and then fainted.

Bright and early, before the crack of dawn, Miss Tatum got out of bed, went over to the pitcher of water and patted the cold water on her face. Standing in front of the full-length mirror, she began to braid her long hair. After dressing, she quietly slipped down the stairs. She took a whiff and peered through the kitchen door.

"Something certainly smells delicious."

There she saw Mr. Staunton and Cotton engaged in a serious conversation.

"Good morning, gentlemen," Miss Tatum said. "I didn't realize Staunton Plantation began before sun up, or I would have set my clock an hour earlier."

Then Mr. Staunton said, "Miss Tatum, this is Mr. Cotton. He'll be your legal advisor while you are here at Staunton.

He knows every aspect of the plantation: boundaries, topographical conditions, seasonal flooding centimeters, and any restricting orders existing on the bordering properties. You will give your daily reports to him. Each night he and I will evaluate your work, and Mr. Cotton will give you instructions for the next day. Do you have any questions?"

"One question…" Miss Tatum stated. "Will I be working alone?"

"No, it's too dangerous in these parts for anyone to work alone," Mr. Staunton replied. "Violence is well-known and occurs quite frequently. Cotton has suggested that three of our ranch hands provide the assistance you will need while here."

Then Miss Tatum responded, "Please allow me to add a few comments. I plan to be here only three days. I plan to work fast, therefore if your so-called ranch hands are dull and complacent, I'd rather work alone. I need no deadbeat distractions, and I'm quite capable of taking care of myself."

Mr. Staunton turned to Cotton. "While Miss Tatum and I are having breakfast, inform Christago that they will be tied up for the next three days, assisting Miss Tatum."

As Carlton looked back at Miss Tatum, he smiled and said, "Young lady, let's just see what you can do. We'll be served now, Cadelia."

After eating breakfast, Mr. Staunton and Leslie walked out on the back balcony. He pulled up a chair for her to be seated. Mr. Staunton was very impressed with Miss Tatum, but his male pride refused to allow him to be complementary to her.

He then asked, "So, just tell me, Miss Tatum, how did a young woman like yourself wind up in a man's world, doing an assignment of this nature?"

"Father always figured I would follow in his steps. He sent me to boarding school out east. I majored in Executive Bookkeeping and Management and Accounting. I thought I was all set."

Mr. Staunton replied, "What happened?"

"I started working out east at a prominent Eastern establishment, The First Commonwealth Banking House in Pennsylvania. I did quite well, I must say. Then I met Jake Starnwell, who introduced me to the man's world of leasing and annexing land properties. Then Jake was offered a promotion out toward Colorado. He picked up lock stock and barrel and relocated himself to the other side of the Colorado River."

"Have you heard from him?" Carlton asked.

"A couple of times," she responded. "He's doing great. He keeps asking me if I'm ready to relocate, but Dad would have a fit if I moved that far away. Besides, I prefer Virginia men. Much easier to deal with, wouldn't you agree, Mr. Staunton?"

"I wouldn't know about that," he quickly answered. Mr. Staunton glanced toward the barn, and Cotton and two young ranch hands were riding toward the back balcony.

Miss Tatum noticed the ranch hands and remarked, "They are young ranch hands, wouldn't you say?"

Mr. Staunton agreed. "I'll admit, most of my men who ride the trails with the Appaloosas are fairly young."

"Over here, Nevada," Carlton called.

The two men rode toward him. Mr. Staunton then introduced Miss Tatum to the men.

"Miss Tatum, I would like you to meet Stacy Sturgeons

– we call him Nevada – and Roddy."

Roddy responded, "Just call me Roddy, ma'am. So glad to make your acquaintance."

Then Cotton spoke up. "The horses are ready, sir, and Christago says the supplies are loaded behind the bunkhouse."

Then Mr. Staunton put his hands on Leslie's shoulders and said, "Miss Tatum – I mean, Leslie – you are in good hands. We will be expecting you all back around dusk."

Leslie smiled at Mr. Staunton, then she looked at the boys and said, "Ready, boys?"

Roddy responded, "We're all set."

Carlton and Leslie walked down the back steps. Carlton helped Leslie onto her horse. Then all three riders headed off in an easterly direction.

The three left the main house heading for the bunkhouse. Nevada motioned for them to follow him. They rode to the back of the bunkhouse. Christago was waiting. He had three large bags. He put two on Nevada's horse and one on Roddy's horse.

Christago then said, "Teddy Gail has packed the lunches. You all be careful. Coyotes are bad around these parts."

Leslie answered back, "We'll be fine, Christago. Two able-bodied men like Roddy and Nevada – we'll be just fine."

Then Roddy responded back to Christago, "Don't expect us back until dusk. The east pasture has never been surveyed, and the map will be difficult to read."

Then Nevada spoke up. "And if we are not back by sundown, come looking."

"Adios," Christago said.

The three riders returned his goodbye in Spanish, and they all started on their way.

Later on that day, the three arrived at a local point where Nevada suggested it was a good spot to begin the surveying. Leslie was on the ground, using her surveying instruments. Accurate measurements were very important to get the precise coverage. They used strings and instruments to measure. Leslie had a pad and pencil with her, and she was writing down each number as they figured it out. The sun was beginning to cross the sky, and the blazing rays began to penetrate their skin.

Then Roddy said, "Miss Tatum, a creek is nearby, a quarter of a mile or so. I suggest we let the horses have a break. They are carrying the bulk of the load, and they do need some relief."

"That's fine, Roddy," Leslie responded. "We could also use a break ourselves. Why don't we plan to eat lunch at that time?"

Nevada remarked, "I'm going to go on and ride ahead. I'll wire the area off, so the horses won't be distracted. You have to be so careful with these horses. They panic so easily, and they will run off. We are way too far to walk back home."

Leslie answered, "Sounds good, Nevada. We'll see you shortly."

Cripple Creek is a perfect little place for lunch. The creek was a winding a little stream where water flowed crystal-clear through the old Virginia wind rocks. Nevada wired off part of the ground so the horses could relax and have easy access to the water supply. Nevada was standing next to a tree. Leslie was sitting on the ground on a blanket, and Roddy was filling the water canteens up. Nevada walked over to Leslie and knelt down. The chili and homemade rolls that Leddy Gail prepared were all the surveyors needed while they took a short relief from their work.

Then Leslie asked, "How long have you fellows been here at Staunton plantation?"

Nevada answered, "I am going on my fifth year, and Roddy just started a couple of months back."

"Do you like the work?" asked Leslie.

Nevada answered, "Can't complain, Mr. Staunton treats us right. Good pay. He's a fair man."

Then Leslie added a compliment to the boys. "Well, nice-looking young men like you all…must be a girl back home."

Roddy spoke up. "Plenty of women in Templeton."

"Yes," Nevada said. "And all of them looking."

Leslie looked puzzled. "Looking?"

"Yeah," Nevada answered. "Looking. Looking for a way to get attached, and I ain't ready for that!"

Roddy spoke up again. "That's why I left Calhoun City. The women was fighting like alley cats. Too much charm will kill a fella, and I must have had it all, 'cause they were all fighting for my attention."

"How far is Templeton from Staunton Plantation?" Leslie asked.

"Fifteen or twenty miles from Staunton," Nevada answered. "Wouldn't you say, Roddy, fifteen or twenty miles?"

Roddy answered, "Probably twenty."

Then Leslie asked, "And that's where Mr. Staunton's

brother works? A Doctor T. D. Staunton?"

"Yes, a fine man," Nevada answered.

Roddy agreed. "The best."

Leslie and the men had finished their chili, then Leslie said, "We best be getting on back to work. We still have several hours before quitting time."

Nevada then spoke up. "And let me be a trite nosy. How is a lovely lady like yourself ever going to enjoy the cultured things of life when you're so involved with trail riding and surveying?"

Leslie put her hand on Nevada's shoulder and said, "Nevada, that's the same question my dad has been asking me for three years now, and I didn't have an answer then and I don't have an answer now. Must be in my blood. I guess a cultured, distinguished man will have to catch me first because I can't slow down to be officially courted."

Later on that night Leslie, Roddy, and Nevada were at the kitchen table, explaining what had been done on the survey work today. They were using a big map showing that acreage of the property.

Cotton looked at the map and said, "No, the flooding washes several yards up that embankment. The sandbagging will not hold it."

Leslie then showed him another location two miles over.

Cotton said, "That will do. Mr. Staunton is not going to pay to have that lot grouped. He calls it wasteland. Disregard it and run the lines Northeast parallel to the bordering boundary!"

Then Leslie said, "That will be a problem."

Before Leslie could finish, Cotton interrupted and said, "No matter — no matter, he'll do the last inspection, and he'll negotiate. Believe me, he knows his property."

Leslie reluctantly replied, "Okay, we'll leave it. When I go back tomorrow, I'll review this again. Against my better judgment, I'm going to consider this alignment."

Cotton responded, "Certainly, certainly, by all means you all go back and look
at this tomorrow. I'll show him the survey measurements thus far. Hopefully, we can look over the layout tomorrow and finish up on Sunday."

"Yes, that's the way I planned it," Leslie remarked. "Goodnight, Mr. Cotton."

As Leslie turned around to leave the kitchen, she nodded to Nevada. "Boys, how about
4:30?"

Roddy answered, "A little early for sunrise service, but we will be ready."

Leslie answered, "Great," and made her way up the stairs. As she sat in front of the beautiful gold ornate framed mirror, she began to imagine all about the late Mrs. Elizabeth Staunton, and the part she played in the whole ramification of the present circumstances. All at once there was a knock on the door.

"It's Rosie, Miss Leslie. Miss Cadelia told me to bring your dinner tray up."

Leslie opened the door, and Rosie left the tray on the end table. Leslie responded by saying, "Thank you, Rosie, I was a bit hungry."

Bright and early the next morning, Leslie was up and dressed and down in the kitchen by
4:15. Much to her surprise, Cadelia was already scurrying around. The bacon, eggs, and grits with homemade

biscuits smelled scrumptious.

Leslie remarked, "Why, Miss Cadelia, you are an amazing woman. No wonder Mr. Staunton watches you like a hawk. You are a wonder woman."

Miss Cadelia replied, "Just doing my job. Taking care of you Stauntons."

Then Leslie questioned, "Are you calling me a Staunton?"

Miss Cadelia smiled and quickly answered, "Not yet, honey, not yet! But I can see the way Mr. Staunton looks at you. I haven't seen that look since Mrs. Elizabeth passed away."

Leslie looked surprised and said, "Really? I can't tell, I really can't tell."

Miss Cadelia gently moved Leslie toward the chair. "Sit down, child. You'll need a hearty
breakfast."

As she started to serve Miss Leslie, in walked Roddy and Nevada.

Roddy said, "We are mighty hungry, Miss Cadelia, mighty hungry."

"Sit down, boys, breakfast is on the table," she replied.

As the boys sat down, Leslie pulled out the map.

"I think we will backtrack today and end up in the north field about dusk."

Cotton said, "Mr. Staunton would not go along with some of the measurements. It won't cut us too short, possibly an hour or so."

Roddy spoke up. "Fine with me."

"It all pays the same," Nevada responded. "Just working two sides of the fence instead of one."

As the three left out the side door from the kitchen, Miss

Cadelia reminded them, "Be
   careful, and we'll look for y'all around dark."
   Leslie said, "Good deal."
   As Leslie walked out, she said, "Appreciate the dinner you sent up last night."
   Miss Cadelia winked at Leslie. "Yes, Mr. Carlton said he knew you needed the nourishment after the full day yesterday."
   Leslie winked back. "Maybe so."
   The three riders were heading toward the east pasture. As the surveyor and two men were taking pictures and measurements, they were talking together and jotting information down on the tablet that Leslie was carrying. They traveled around the property to several locations, surveying the land. The three seemed very pleased with the accomplishments they had made. Taking time out for a quick lunch, they stopped near the other end of the Cripple Creek embankment. Nevada was filling up the canteens. Roddy was getting the horses watered. They had already picked up all the litter that had been made from lunch. The sausage and fried beans had been very tasty. Roddy made sure the fire was out before they left the location. These dry, hot summer days were very hazardous for spreading of wildfires. Roddy noticed that Leslie had gotten back on her horse, and for some reason or another the horse was disturbed quite a bit. The horse went round and round and round, then he began to buck up, as though he were really frightened.
   Nevada hollered, "Hold the reins tight, Leslie, he's trying to get away!"
   The horse bucked three or four times, then began to

stomp furiously at the ground. When Miss Leslie looked down, a cotton mouth water moccasin was wrapped around the horse's leg and was making its way toward Leslie's leg. Leslie tried to strike the snake with the surveying instrument, but she lost balance and fell off the horse. With all this commotion, the snake withdrew itself from Champion and slid on back into the water swamp. Thank the Lord, Champion was not harmed. Roddy and Nevada ran to Leslie. When they got to her she could not stand up.

The following day, everybody was back at the big house. Leslie's father has come to Staunton Plantation just to check on his daughter. Dr. Staunton had checked Leslie over thoroughly and was very satisfied with her condition.

Carlton was talking with her father. "It does look like she'll be all right, but it was a close call."

"I do believe I'll stay overnight," Mr. Tatum replied. "And I'll take the train on back in the morning. I'm going on to my room. Tell Cadelia to send my plate up."

As he turned to go to his room, he said, "I'm glad your sister will be here tomorrow. You will really need the extra help, while Leslie is recuperating and regaining her strength. I'm just so thankful. It's been hard on me. Lida Mae passed last year. It has been extremely difficult, but the thoughts of losing Leslie were almost unbearable. I'm going on to bed, Carlton. See you in the morning."

Carlton put his arm around him and assured him, "She'll be all right. She'll need to rest, but we can handle that." Then Leslie's father, Edgar, said, "Thanks for everything."

Carlton mentioned again, "Cadelia will be up with dinner shortly."

The next morning Carlton was walking into the kitchen

when he noticed Miss Cadelia.

"Morning, Miss Cadelia," he said. "My, you look awfully spiffy this morning. That new fella, Mr. Rossetti, must be coming on strong."

Then Miss Cadelia quickly responded, "Whatever gave you such a notion?"

Carlton replied, "Only the new hairdo and the bright new dress and the radiant smile. I haven't seen that smile in over a year. Yes, need I say more? That Mr. Rossetti is definitely coming on strong."

Cadelia turned away from Mr. Staunton and said, "Enough of that! Why don't you take Miss Tatum's breakfast on up? Do encourage her to eat the grits and ham hocks. She is so thin and frail. She really needs to fatten up a little, as she regains her strength. You might also mention to her that your brother will be checking by this afternoon. He'll be taking one of his patients to Calhoun City this morning. He's not fully equipped to handle the situation, and he didn't want to take any chances on this lady's recovery, so he'll be by some time this afternoon."

"Breakfast looks awfully appetizing, Cadelia, why don't you prepare another breakfast plate and send it up, and we will eat together on the porch."

Cadelia responded, "Sure thing, Mr. Staunton. By the way, you know your sister will be arriving at noon tomorrow."

"I'm glad you reminded me," Carlton replied. "Ted has surgery planned for tomorrow, and he'll be out most of the day. We knew Martha was arriving, but I was not sure of the time."

"Thelma sent word last night that her name was on the

passenger list," said Cadelia. "The train is to arrive at 12:30."

"Well, that's perfect timing!" he responded. "You know Ted and I are going to Washington in a couple of weeks. We could be out for several weeks. I'm glad she's finally arriving. Jessica Leigh needs to get started reviewing the calculus and physics before she takes those placement exams. Wilshire is such a strict academy."

Mr. Staunton picked up the silver tray and walked up the stairway to Miss Tatum's room. He would never admit the fond attraction he had for this young lady. He knocked softly, then opened the door. As he entered the room, he saw that he had interrupted Leslie and her father as they were talking.

"Oh," he said. "I am sorry, Edgar, I didn't realize you were still here."

Then Carlton put the breakfast tray down.

Edgar replied, "Just saying my goodbyes, Carlton."

He kissed her on the cheek and said, "I know she is in good hands." Leslie grabbed her father's hand and said, "Dad, please don't worry. I'll be up and around and back to my spunky self by the end of the week."

Mr. Staunton interrupted. "I don't know about that. Ted seems to think you'll have to be off your leg at least two and a half to three weeks."

Leslie answered, "Whatever, Dad. I'm in good hands. I'm sure you'll have some consultations and executive meetings back home. We all know the bank cannot run without your bodily assistance, even though you are retired. So please don't miss your train, and I'll see you soon. You are still my most favorite gentleman caller and always will be."

Mr. Tatum hugged and kissed his daughter again. "Okay, sugar, I'm off."

Edgar then shook Carlton's hand and said, "I'm leaving her with you. I'll see myself out and call in a few days."

"We'll patch her up and send her back as good as new," Carlton responded.

As Mr. Tatum was leaving, Carlton said to Leslie, "Cadelia is bringing up my breakfast. Would you like to join me on the balcony, and we can eat breakfast together?"

"That would be nice," she answered.

As Miss Cadelia brought in the second food tray, she smiled. "Did you sleep all right, missy?"

"Yes ma'am, just fine," she responded. Then Cadelia handed the tray to Carlton, and then she exited the room. Carlton took both trays to the outside porch. Then he returned and helped Miss Tatum onto the wheelchair. Then he pushed her onto the gallery.

Leslie exclaimed, "Oh, it's so beautiful out here. Mr. Staunton, this is such a lovely view! When I arrived, the West Wing room did not have an enchanting view like this one."

Mr. Staunton exclaimed, "Yes, it's a breathtaking view. This was my wife's favorite room. She furnished all of the other rooms in the house, but she hired a French designer to decorate this room. He spent two months with us, and she and Monsieur Sier chose all of the elaborate prints and fabrics. They imported all of the furnishings from shops in Paris and London. Yes, she loved this room. She would spend hours and hours painting and writing poetry. She gazed out the windows, admiring the beautiful gardens. She claimed the gardens are what gave her inspiration for her poetry and paintings."

Leslie agreed with Carlton. "I can see how this is like a fairytale, and one could easily feel like a princess just by being in this room. If I close my eyes, I can pretend I'm in a castle. All I have to do is make a wish, and everything will come true. You actually feel like a fairytale heroine." Carlton began to feel he had talked too much about his wife, and he began to close back up to his cold, reserved self. He brought both trays of breakfast out on the gallery and put the trays on a small table. The two of them ate silently, while Leslie gazed out on the beautiful gardens. As they were enjoying the food, Leslie could not help but wonder what was Elizabeth Staunton really like.

Interrupting her train of thought, Carlton addressed her again. "Leslie, my sister Martha is arriving today. She'll be tutoring Jessica Leigh in her studies."

"Yes," Miss Tatum added. "Jessica told me she was going to Wilshire in the fall. Isn't that a little expensive?"

Mr. Staunton quickly admitted, "Yes, as a matter of fact, it is very expensive, but her mother was a graduate of that school. Elizabeth always planned for Jessica to attend, and Jessica seems to be quite excited about going."

"Oh, is she?" Leslie questioned. "How can you tell?"

Carlton abruptly replied, "Why wouldn't she be? It is the best girls finishing school in the east."

When Elizabeth left Wilshire, she was equipped and educated to attend any college in the world."

"Well?" Leslie asked. "Just where did she go?"

Stuttering, Carlton replied, "Nowhere, she married me."

Tired of talking, Leslie nodded her head and told Carlton, "I'm awfully tired, will you please roll me back to bed?

I do feel rather faint with all this conversation."

He rolled her back to her room and helped her into the bed. He then took the two trays downstairs and knew in his heart that he must have bombed out.

CHAPTER 5

Native American History Lesson

It was 5:30 a.m. in the bunkhouse. Leddy Gail was preparing breakfast for the black workers on the plantation. Leddy Gail was at the stove, and Cotton, Tommy Toes, and several other adults were moving around, trying to get dressed and get ready for the day's chores.

Leddy Gail exclaimed, "Cotton, are you going to warn the girls?"

"Warn them about what?" Cotton replied.

Then Leddy Gail quickly responded, "Aberdeen Cotton, don't play nanny with me. You know good and dang well, the skeletal skull has magical powers. I thought you buried that skull in Alligator Swamp last year."

"He did, Leddy Gail," Tommy Toes interjected. "He did bury it."

Leddy Gail quickly looked at Tommy Toes. "How do you know? Did you see him bury it?"

"Well," Tommy Toes admitted. "I didn't actually see him bury it."

"That's what I thought. Now, when people start

disappearing, and the cattle start vanishing, and the moon don't come out for several days, then you'll know for sure we done disturbed the Indian Goddess of Revolution again. She'll be after us to return that baby skull."

Tommy Toes questioned, "What did we do last year? It was so strange, but it satisfied the

Indian gods, and they left us alone."

Rosie moved over to the big table. "Did I miss something?" she asked.

"Naw," Cotton told her. "You didn't miss nuttin."

Leddy Gail and Cadelia decided it was best to speak little of the baby skull and handle the problem themselves.

"The legend goes back to ancient civilization," Tommy Toes interrupted. "A Cherokee

Indian princess had a baby. Custom was to put the baby to death, 'cause they couldn't find who the daddy was."

Then Leddy Gail spoke up to clear up the situation. "The princess refused to tell the Indian warriors who the father was, for fear he was a white man. So, the princess protected her baby by sending him to another Indian tribe located somewhere in the Mississippi Delta. I was only a small girl, and I was working at Claremont Plantation at the time. I knowed they had taken in a small Indian boy, a half-breed. He did not make it. He was so little and so pale, but even back then it was hearsay that he had magical powers from the Indian gods. Most of us black folks stayed clear, 'cause Lord only knows we didn't need no superstitions against us."

Then Rosie spoke up. "Please continue."

Tommy Toes acknowledged the fact, saying, "Well, we all just forgot about the child. Most of us followed Mr.

Staunton on up here and tried to get on with our lives."

"Then about three years ago…" Leddy Gail remembered. "There was five or six Indian men from Cherokee, North Carolina. They were selling horses or something."

"Yeah," Tommy Toes noted. "They was selling baskets, belts, Indian wares, and whatever. They stopped in Calhoun City. The hotel would not put them up for the night, so Ted Staunton wired his brother, and the red men came on out to Staunton Plantation. They stayed the rest of the week. We all got to go meet the men."

"As a matter of fact…" Leddy Gail said. "Tommy Toes, you and Christago became very familiar with them. However, it was strange. The men kept asking us about the little boy from Claremont. Cotton must have mentioned the half-breed to them, and the questions started flying. It wasn't until after they were gone, we discovered a handwritten ancient archaeological research finding that explained the disappearance of the authentic Babylonian skull. It was a baby, half-Indian and half-Egyptian. The skull did have magical, satanic, and spiritual powers. The custom was that when the princess desired the powers of the child, she would inhabit the premises until she found the baby's submissiveness. This may take weeks. Once she conquered the child, the baby would vanish for years. Both of these two were very present in living and dead origins in the world."

Rosie almost laughed out loud. "Now don't tell me that you folks believe in ghosts!"

Leddy Gail shrieked, "I do, and I always will! When a spiritual being wants its way, I guarantee you she will win, no matter who you are."

Tommy Toes spoke up again. "I remember now. We had to wrap the baby skull in animal skins. Then we had to soak it in raisin berries and brine, and then we had to take the skull out to Alligator Swamp for that ritualistic burial."

Rosie was puzzled. "I do not understand. How did you all know about the ancient authentic burial procedure?"

"It was written in yellow ink, and the document gave specific detailed instructions," said Leddy Gail. "It clearly said follow everything to a 't'. "

Rosie was so impatient that she pushed Leddy Gail to continue the story. "So what happens next?"

Leddy Gail answered, "The strange events ceased. Several of our men folks were found outside state lines. They were not harmed, but they had no recollection of how they got there or how long they had been gone."

"So," Rosie put in. "They just came home and picked up where they left off?"

Leddy Gail just nodded. Then Cotton said, "Tell her about the cattle."

"Well, it seems like the day was mighty windy," Cotton started. "And the heavy winds blowed several hundred head of cattle past Cripple Creek and set them down outside north of Templeton. It was a strange occurrence, the strangest I ever did see."

"Not strange at all," Leddy Gail argued. "The Indian princess put out her demands, and we Blacks had to oblige, huh…and it looks like we may be faced with the same situation all over, with this baby Indian skull showing up again."

CHAPTER 6

Aunt Martha Arrives

This was the morning Aunt Martha was to arrive. Jessie was at the breakfast table, eating her lunch. Cadelia was moving around in the kitchen.

Carlton came in and said, "Pumpkin, you ready to go?"

Jessica jumped up and Cadelia interrupted, "Not yet, young lady. That hickory smoked ham is just waiting for a hungry young lady. We don't want Aunt Martha to think we don't feed folks around here, especially you. Mister Carlton, you are as thin as skin and bones. Maybe Aunt Martha can fatten you up. I can't seem to."

Jessica looked at her father. "I'm through, Dad. Do I look okay? I want Aunt Martha to see how much I've grown."

Mr. Carlton smiled and nodded his head. "Fine, Pumpkin, the wagon is out front."

The next scene was in Templeton. Mr. Staunton, Jessica Leigh, and Calcutta went into the bank.

Carlton walked over to the window and talked to the banker. "Storms out West must have delayed the train."

The banker answered, "Yep, the radio announced heavy storms with hail."

Then Mr. Lehman looked at the west window.

Carlton reminded him, "You know Martha is expected in today."

"Yeah," Mr. Lehman answered. "I saw her name on the passenger list. I've got her account all made out. Transferring her account from San Bernardino has been no trouble at all, no trouble at all, Carlton."

All at once, Jessica Leigh ran into the bank, screaming, "Dad, Dad, the train is coming!"

Then she ran out to catch the train. Carlton looked at Mr. Lehman. "Thanks for everything. Let me catch up with Jessica."

The train pulled up into the depot. Mr. Staunton and Jessica Lee were waiting inside. The storm began to blow in. The passengers began to get off. An old woman and two small children got off. Then a slim, dark-haired lady was walking toward the station. The dark rimmed glasses made it very hard to tell who she was. Her dark hair was balled up in a bun, and her old-fashioned, plaid, pleated skirt made it quite obvious this was Aunt Martha, and she had arrived.

Mr. Staunton briskly walked toward her and kissed her and gave her a big hug.

"Why, Carly," Aunt Martha scolded him. "You are so thin. Cadelia told me you had almost dried up. She said you simply refuse to eat."

Jessica waited patiently then spoke up. "What about me, Aunt Martha?"

Aunt Martha bent over and hugged Jessica Leigh really hard. "Pumpkin, you are a head taller and the spittin' image of your mother."

Aunt Martha looked up at Carlton and said, "My brother,

you no longer have a rambunctious, rowdy girl. She is now a beautiful young lady, and I know Elizabeth would be so very proud of her."

Aunt Martha bent over and hugged her again. Jessica Leigh was grinning like a possum, and she took Aunt Martha's hand.

As they were heading toward the wagon, Aunt Martha turned around to Carlton. "The brown plaid luggage is mine and don't forget those two hat boxes."

Aunt Martha then whispered to Carlton, "One is for Jessica Leigh. I bought the matching fabric. I figured I would get our girl all fixed up for school."

Carlton smiled, "Sounds good to me."

Then he went into the luggage room and picked up the plaid luggage and the two hat boxes and walked out to the wagon. Aunt Martha petted and greeted Calcutta, and they all start on the way home.

As they were riding in the wagon, Aunt Martha was sitting next to Carlton, and Jessica Leigh was on the bench in the back of the wagon.

Aunt Martha asked, "Where is Ted?"

Carlton responded, "In Calhoun City. He said he and the children would be over later on tonight."

As the wagon pulled up in front of the house, Christago hobbled out to the wagon.

"Buenos días, Señora Martha. Glad to have you back." He picked up the luggage and carried it into the parlor. Aunt Martha greeted him back and said, "Muy bien, Señor Christago, I'm glad to be back."

"Dad," Jessica Leigh explained. "Calcutta and I are going out to the south pasture. I've only a few weeks left before I have to go to school, and Calcutta and I need some valuable time together."

Mr. Staunton answered her back, saying, "Be home by sundown. You know Uncle Ted's joining us for dinner. Be sure you return in time to freshen up. We want our first dinner together to be a nice one."

Jessica went over to Aunt Martha and told her again how glad she was that she had come.

She then kissed her on the cheek. She got out of the wagon, went to the barn and bridled up Patches and the three of them, Jessica Leigh, Calcutta and Patches, rode off to the south pasture. About three miles deep into the thick wooded brush, Jessica Leigh had a clubhouse. The clubhouse was in an old oak tree. Agnes, George, Sabrina and Jessica Leigh spent many hours playing in the treehouse. Whenever Jessica Leigh was lonely or sad, she would ride out to the treehouse and she and Calcutta would work it all out. How she loved the treehouse, and how she loved Calcutta. She knew that within a few short weeks she would be on train headed for Wilshire Academy.

Meanwhile, back at the big house, when Aunt Martha and Carlton arrived, Cadelia warmly approached Aunt Martha. She hugged her affectionately and said, "Welcome."

"Ladies," Carlton interjected, as he turned to Aunt Martha. "Sis, Cadelia will help you with everything you need. I have some important documents to go get ready for Washington."

Cadelia then spoke up again. "Ted sent word. He reminded me that they would be running late. Said he had been in the clinic all afternoon, and the paperwork has to be completed for his patient. You know, Mr. Staunton, with your brother, his practice always comes first."

"He has always been so dedicated," Martha added. "However, I'm just afraid perhaps that the children have been somewhat neglected."

Carlton questioned, "What do you mean, Martha?"

"Well," Martha explained, "Agnes is too grown up, if you know what I mean. George has no backbone for a young man his age, and Sabrina is simply too rowdy and rambunctious. I just believe if Teddy had put the children in the right priority, his youngsters would be – how do you say it? – more wholesome and cultured. Never you mind, Carlton, I'm here now, and any family problems we all have, I can solve. I'm just hoping I'm not too late for Agnes. I'm sure I can handle others, but I may be a year or two behind on changing that young lady."

"I do wish you luck," Carlton acknowledged her and added, "Teddy has had rounds and rounds with that child. She thinks she is grown up, and she is so stubborn. Besides, she is as smart as a whip. That's what makes it so hard. She can outthink him two to one and come out the winner every time. She's hard on all of us. Let me be excused, Sis."

Then he turned to Cadelia. "I'll see you ladies at dinner." He exited the library. Aunt Martha and Cadelia exited to the kitchen.

Cadelia expressed her happiness, saying, "I'm so glad you're here. I can only do so much with your brother. He is so busy. The Washington trip is so important. The president has called twice. Ted and Carlton both have been placed on the steering committee. The president says a war on wages is the only profitable solution, and if the Russians provide artillery with ammunition, we are doomed. Both men are under a lot of stress. Martha, I can handle Staunton Plantation, but I cannot handle the world affairs, and the Lord is seemingly falling on the Southern tobacco plantation owners. I cringe to think about another war, but it seems inevitable."

"Cadelia," Aunt Martha explained. "The Lord is on our side. We have strong, brilliant men who are accustomed to strategy combat. All we women have to do is provide our encouragement, along with tender care."

"Sounds so simple when you talk," Cadelia noted.

"Miss Martha, I want to believe that it's only a matter of time before things will be back to normal."

Aunt Martha then interrupted, saying, "Possibly never as it was, but hopefully the new day will bring new happiness as we have never experienced before."

As the ladies were talking, in walked Miss Tatum. She was on crutches.

"Am I interrupting?" she asked.

Turning around, Cadelia said, "Oh no, honey, Miss Leslie Tatum, it gives me pleasure to introduce you to Mr. Staunton's sister, Martha Sturdivant. Miss Sturdivant, Leslie is our houseguest. She was doing some survey work for Mr. Staunton when her horse was frightenedby a water moccasin. She fell off and broke her leg in the accident. Dr. Teddy is treating her. She should be back on her feet in a couple of weeks."

Miss Tatum was shocked. "Surely you can't mean that long? Why, I figured I would be back on my feet by the end of this week? There is no way I can be out that long. I have commitments."

Then Leslie turned to Martha. "It is nice to meet you. Mr. Staunton has spoken of you. He seems very pleased that you have come to help them out. I will not be in your way."

Aunt Martha reassured Leslie, "My brother has always had houseguests, and I can assure you, he does not think you being here will cause any interference with his daily activities or work. As a matter of fact, I have a feeling he is enjoying your company."

"Well," Leslie remarked. "I do believe I'll go back upstairs. Again, nice meeting you, Miss Sturdivant."

Then Miss Tatum turned and went back upstairs to her room.

The treehouse had two levels. The first level was easy to get to. All you had to do was walk up three wooden planks, and you were on the first floor. The first floor was three-by-five feet. Walking up five more planks, you could reach the second level. The second level was a smaller floor space, being a three-by-three-foot room. When Jessica Leigh was with Calcutta, they stayed on the first level. With her arms around Calcutta, she was very sad.

"I love you, Calcutta," she whispered in his ear. She even kissed him on the nose, and his tail began to wag. Tears began to stream down her face.

"I can't bear to leave you."

Calcutta sensed something was wrong. He began to whimper.

"Don't cry, boy, don't cry. I am doing enough crying for both of us," she tried to explain.

Jessica continued to hold him in her arms. Her train of

thought was aroused when she heard the sound of a wagon in the distance.

Jumping up, Jessica exclaimed, "It must be Uncle Teddy!"

She and Calcutta hurriedly jumped down from the tree-house and followed the path back toward the main house, running all the way. By the time she got to the end of the path, she saw Uncle Teddy and the three children heading toward the house.

"Hey, wait up!" she hollered.

Uncle Teddy stopped the wagon. Jessica and Calcutta hopped on, and all of them rode toward the house.

The big table was set in the dining room. Cadelia had planned a very elegant meal for Aunt Martha's first night. The Royal Daulton and silver goblets were on the table. Rosie had been polishing the silver all morning, while Cadelia and Samantha had been in the kitchen preparing the food. When Dr. Staunton arrived, the family was all seated in the parlor.

Carlton told Jessica, "Go upstairs and wash up for dinner. We will wait on you."

When Jessica came down, the family proceeded to the dining hall. Ted and Carlton always sat at each end of the table. Leslie was next to Ted, and George was on the other side of Ted. Jessica Leigh was on one side of Carlton. Martha was on the other side. Agnes was in between George, and Aunt Martha was between Leslie and Jessica Leigh.

After Carlton said grace, Cadelia and Rosie began to bring the food in on silver trays, serving each of the guests.

"Why, Cadelia, you and Rosie have outdone yourselves. I do not think I've ever seen a prettier table setting!" Aunt Martha bragged.

"Well," Carlton responded. "You are always a special guest at our house. Ted and I always look forward to your visit. However, of course," Ted added. "We do miss your husband."

"Of course, you all know he was not well enough to make the long trip," Martha explained. "Besides, he knew I would be here several months, and he does not need to be away his doctors."

"And how is his condition?" Teddy inquired.

"About the same. You remember he had a minor stroke. He seems to be getting along quite well, and, of course, he has two sisters who live in the same town, and they check on him daily. So, I know he is in good hands."

Then Dr. Staunton noticed Miss Leslie. "And how are you doing, Miss Tatum?"

"Quite well, Dr. Staunton, and thank you for asking. I know I'm ready to return home, but my father assured me I would have to get approval from you before I leave Staunton Plantation."

"Young lady," Teddy said. "I'll be in to see you about the middle of next week to check on your progress. Cadelia tells me you are doing quite well."

"Wait one minute," Carlton spoke up. "Miss Tatum is not leaving this house until I am satisfied with her condition myself. Her father is really holding me responsible for her recovery, and she will not leave until I am sure she is ready to go."

Leslie had a disgusted look on her face, but secretly she was smiling inside. She really enjoyed being here at Staunton, and she was really fond of Carlton. But trying to hold her composure, she didn't say another word.

"Aunt Martha," Carlton addressed her attention. "Ted and I are going to Washington for several weeks on business."

"When are you leaving?" asked Aunt Martha.

"Probably the end of the month," he replied. "I'm sure everything will be fine here at home. You and Miss Cadelia are so efficient."

"And of course..." Carlton added. "The farm business will certainly be left in reputable hands. The men here can run this place as well as I can."

"I do not know about that," Ted interrupted. "Don't fret, Ted, I'll leave explicit instructions for everyone to carry out. I'm not worried one bit."

Then Carlton added, "Don't you remember? Ted, last year we were gone two weeks, and everything went fine."

"Yes, but it was not in the middle of the tobacco crop coming in," Ted muttered. Again, Carlton reassured him, "Everything will be fine. I trust all of our ranch hands and crop workers. Besides, if any problems arise, we can be here in a matter of days. Enough business, enough business. Miss Cadelia, we are ready for dessert."

So, Miss Cadelia and Rosie brought the bread pudding and coffee, and all enjoyed the rest of the meal.

CHAPTER 7

Is Cotton Dead?

Late that night, after the first meal with Aunt Martha was over, all was quiet in the main house at Staunton Plantation, all the lights were out, and all the dishes were done. Must've been around 12 a.m. or so, there was a loud hollering, and someone was beating on Miss Cadelia's back door. When she heard the banging, she turned on the kerosene lamp and opened the back door. Opening the heavy door, she saw Leddy Gail trying to open the screen door and waving her hands.

"He's dead, Miss Cadelia, he's dead, Cotton is dead!"

Cadelia tried to quiet Leddy Gail. "Hush up, Leddy Gail, hush up, you'll wake up the whole household."

In a quieter tone, Leddy Gail tried to explain. "Rosie and Samantha been prowling around Alligator Swamp again. Rosie been a courtin' an uptown Negro after dark. This been going on for some time now. If we had known what was going on, we would have killed them boys, if we could have catched urn."

Then Cadelia asked, "So, what does that have to do with Cotton?"

Leddy Gail stammered to Cadelia, "You knows about his private business, don't you?"

Nodding, Cadelia admitted, "I have known for some time, but I've tried to stay out of it. I knowed the less I know the better."

Leddy Gail continued. "Mr. Cotton is chained to a cypress tree in Alligator Swamp. Samantha didn't know if he was dead or not. Rosie and her fellow was spending time as they usually do in the back woods. Samantha waited for them on the swamp bank as usual, when she saw Cotton's red flannel shirt."

"Where is Samantha now?" Cadelia questioned.

Leddy Gail screamed, "She's in the cabin washing up! She tried to move him, but the red blood gushed out from his side. Then she was afraid to move him, so she ran home. She never did find Rosie or that Negro boy, whatever his name was. So, she just ran home and told me."

"Miss Cadelia, Miss Cadelia, what we gonna do?" Leddy Gail pleaded. She quickly responded, "Get Christago to hitch up the wagon. I'll fetch Roddy and Nevada. Get me a bed ready in the bunkhouse. Don't wake the children, and please keep this to yo'self, at least till morning."

Cadelia was very glad to have Aunt Martha here. This gave her a chance to slip off during the day, and go down to the old bunkhouse to check on Cotton. The old bunkhouse was only a few yards from the newer ones. When Mr. Staunton had the old home place remodeled, he doubled the living quarters for the Negroes. He added two cabins, rather than the one single component. The old wooden shack was now used for a storage bin, but Cadelia knew it was clean enough for a bed for Cotton. It was extremely important to try to keep the talk down.

Cadelia did not know what had happened at Alligator Swamp or why it had happened, but she knew it was serious–serious enough that she may have to contact White Feather. She could not take any chances and run the risk of losing any of her people. White Feather had to be notified before it was too late. The warning signal was given only once, then the evacuation. Cadelia knew she must act quickly. The Apache baby skull had satanic powers, and they were starting to disperse themselves. Cadelia knew she had to try to talk to Cotton. Heaven only knew what this was all about.

Personally, Cadelia hoped that the private business of Cotton was the culprit. Heaven forbid; if it had anything to do with the baby Indian skull, we would all be in a lot of trouble. When Cadelia finally arrived at the bunkhouse, the men had already gone to Alligator Swamp, unchained Cotton, and brought him back to the cabin. Leddy Gail had put fresh linens on the cot. Cotton's old, red flannel shirt, which had been drenched with blood, had been washed and was hanging on the rack near the fireplace. His trousers were laying near the cot, and the blood was still oozing from his chest and shoulders. Cadelia went over to Cotton, shook him several times to get him to respond.

"Who did this to you, who did this to you?"

Cotton moaned and groaned several times. He tried to open his eyes, but the pain was too severe. Cadelia motioned to Leddy Gail to bring a clean cloth and whiskey. She poured the whiskey over the wound, and Cotton hollered, then passed out.

"We have got to get Dr. Staunton," Cadelia shrieked.

Leddy Gail gulped. "But, but—"

Cadelia argued back, "But, but I don't care; if we don't get help, he will certainly die. Tell Samantha to go get Mr. Staunton. I'll take care of the rest."

Several minutes later, Carlton appeared at the bunk-house cabin.

"What's he doing down here?" Carlton asked.

"I knew he needed to rest," Cadelia answered. "And it's quiet, so I had Leddy Gail fix the cot."

"So, what happened?" Carlton inquired again.

"Well…" Cadelia responded. "He was fooling around at the curing shed. Something had gone wrong with the ventilation hood. He was working on the heater. He didn't have the ladder locked, so it fell. He fell over thirty feet from the top of the shed on to those metal plates."

"Here, let me take a look," Carlton said. "Looks pretty bad. There's some medicine in the main house. I'll get Teddy to come down here when he is treating Leslie tomorrow. I'll come with him, and he can take a look. Meanwhile, send Samantha back to the main house, and I'll get the medicine for you all."

"Thanks, Mr. Carlton," Cadelia added. "Thank you so much. Christago tried to warn him about that old ladder, but he wouldn't listen. You know Mr. Cotton…"

"Yeah, Cadelia," Carlton responded. "I know Cotton. He thinks he can do anything, but we'll have him fixed up real soon. Be sure someone is down here with him all night. Don't leave him alone."

"Where's Samantha?" Carlton questioned.

"Here I is." She quickly appeared.

"Come with me, Samantha, and you can bring the

medicine back to Cadelia."

"Yaw, sir."

The two of them walked back to the big house. Cadelia tried to arouse Cotton again.

"Now, Aberdeen Cotton, wake up, you sorry Negro! What really happened?"

"Hell!" he hollered. "I don't know what you mean."

"You don't know!" she interrupted. "What was you doing in the Alligator Swamp to begin with? Answer me the truth!"

"Well, er, well, er..." He finally acknowledged the truth. "You knows about my business, my private business, don't you? Well, er, every time the boys get the barrels ready to cross the state line, some hombres shows up and puts bullet holes in our kegs. So, I figures I'd go check it out myself. I was down at the stills, coming back on the old short road. I checked the wagons myself, knowing the holes was not in the kegs. All at once, somebody came from behind, blindfolded me, hit me on the head, and next thing I know, I was chained to a tree and blindfolded. I figured it was those hombres."

"Why would they do that?" Cadelia asked.

"Well, they got they own stills two miles down the road, and I am guessing they don't want to share the profits. That's all I can figures. But, Cadelia, it was strange because..."

He hesitated, and Cadelia snapped back at him, "Why was it strange?"

Cotton continued, "For several hours, I lay there. I smelled smoke. I could hear rustling in the brush. I could smell the fire burning, but I could hear bones, bones, more bones, rattling bones."

"What happened to your chest?" she addressed him again.

"Lordy, Cadelia," he said. "I thought I was a goner. A sharp object slashed several gashes on my chest—not too deep, just deep enough to draw blood. Then I began to feel sharp objects cutting my shoulder blades. Each cut drew more blood, 'til I was covered with my own blood."

"Who was talking? What was being said?" Cadelia asked.

"Nothing, nobody said a word! All I could hear was beating drums in the background and those rustling bones, all clacking together. Then, I guess, I must have passed out, cause'n I don't remember nothing else. That is, 'til the boys brought me back to the cabin."

Cadelia gazed at Cotton. "Do you think?"

"Yeah, Cadelia. I'm afraid them Indians are looking for the baby skull, and we better contact White Feather immediately."

Cadelia quickly agreed, "I think so, too. I'll send Rooster into town tomorrow. Dr. Staunton is coming out in the morning to see you. Can you stick to the story I told Mr. Staunton?"

"Yes, Cadelia. I heard every word you said," Cotton replied, "And, believe me, I can lie rather than tell what I think really happened."

"Good," she said, adding, "Keep it amongst the black folks."

All at once, Samantha opened the door with the medicine.

"Samantha," Cadelia said. "Get back to the cabin and keep yo' mouth shut. Since'n you are the one totally responsible for bringing the baby skull back in our lives."

"But..." Samantha tried to express herself. "I can explain."

"Explain nuttin'. Rosie told me she told you to take the skull to Alligator Swamp, and you didn't do what she told you to do. So, young lady, I hold you totally responsible for this calamity. Get back to the cabin and keep yo' mouth shut."

The next morning, Ms. Cadelia was busy with her daily chores, but she was unable to concentrate. She knew the baby's skull meant trouble, and lots of it. The last time we had a bout with those Indians, White Feather contacted his ancestors and negotiated and solved the spiritual conflict, and it was appearing like they would have to contact him again to get the problem solved. White Feather and a few followers of his ran a small trading post located at the end of town. They sold mostly baskets, furs, tools, and trinkets made by the local tribes still in the area. White Feather was a very peaceful, considerate, pleasant, and intelligent Red Man, and all people around Staunton, Virginia liked and respected him. Every time Ms. Cadelia dealt with White Feather, she sent Rooster. Rooster was a light-skinned, black man with bright red hair. He seemed to be a little off, but those Red Men related very well to him. Ms. Cadelia had always thought Rooster could act and behave any way he wanted to. How he acted seemed to depend entirely on the circumstances. And, most of the time, he appeared to be a little off. But, like I said, Cadelia believed it was all an act, and he played his part well, according to the circumstances he found himself in at the time.

If there was a new woman brought in to help on the

plantation, Rooster played the Casanova role and usually charmed the britches off the new lady. Then Mr. Staunton and Dr. Teddy always depended on Rooster to take care of the young'uns. All the children loved him, black and white. He could entertain them for hours, telling tales of his past – mostly lies, of course, but nonetheless they were very entertaining. If either man, Mr. Carlton or Dr. Teddy, needed the children to be taken somewhere, they always called on Rooster. Yes, Rooster had really made a place for himself on Staunton Plantation, simply by doing what he did best, and that means simply doing what he wanted to do, whenever he wanted to do it. But some have it made, and others don't. Occasionally, Rooster would trim the roses or paint the back fence.

Oh, well enough complaining about what he did or didn't do. He could converse with White Feather, and that was exactly what had to be done to solve this situation.

Ms. Cadelia left the kitchen, walked out to the pantry, and motioned for Rosie to come to her. Rosie had been scrubbing floors.

"Rosie," Ms. Cadelia said. "Go get Rooster. Send him to Leddy Gail. Leddy Gail will give him instructions. Looks like he'll have to make another visit to White Feather."

"Is it about that baby skull?" Rosie asked.

"You guessed it. I figured Cotton was attacked. The spirit must have gotten angry again."

"Yes ma'am," Rosie answered eagerly. "I'll go right away."

CHAPTER 8

White Feather's Instruction

Rooster was in the wagon, heading toward Calhoun City. The clouds were beginning to look a little dark. Lord only knows how many black folks are scared to death of bad weather, and with the old Indian spirits mad about the missing baby skull, there was just no telling what type of weather distractions those Redskins could dream up.

Rooster said to himself, "I better get to Calhoun City before them Injuns get the hint that I'm trying to get to White Feather before they do. If I don't hurry, they will destroy me before I can get there."

Rooster was talking out loud to himself, as his wagon hurriedly rolled on to Calhoun City. As Rooster looked backwards, he began to whip the horse faster because the storm was beginning to pick up speed. Then the rain began to pour. The lightning began to strike, and the thunder began to roar. Thank goodness White Feather's trading post was on this side of Calhoun City. Two Indians were propped up on the porch, and three more Indians were seated around a small table smoking cigarettes. All of the men were watching as the storm blew in. The water was pouring down so fast, you could hardly see. All at once, the Indians on the porch spied a figure in the distance coming toward town.

The Indians stood up and began to holler as loudly as they could, "This way! This way, quick!" Then a flash of lightning lit up the sky, and a bolt of thunder rocked the trading post.

"Man, I'm going in. We could all get killed waiting on that wagon," stated one of the

Indians.

Then all the men stepped inside the trading post.

"What's happening?" White Feather inquired.

One of the Indians went over to White Feather. White Feather was seated on an old, cowhide rocker. He was just rocking. That's what he did practically every day. Last year he had a stroke. He didn't injure his mental abilities, but he couldn't walk without assistance.

The Indians bent over and hollered into White Feather's ear, "I know you can't hear well, but you bound to see the storm clouds overhead, hovering over Calhoun City and the lightning, you bound to see the lightning when it brightens up the whole sky."

White feather remarked, "Bad weather…been predicted three days. Just wondered when it would come over."

"Well, it's here" the Indian announced. "It's finally here!"

"He's coming in, he's coming in!" they hollered. All of the Indians had been watching for the figure in the wagon, who was fighting the rainstorm to come into town. The wagon was making its way to the Indian trading post. As

Rooster got nearer, the Indians all went out to help him. He needed their help out of the wagon and into the trading post.

"Who is it?" White Feather inquired. The other Indians helped White Feather up out of

his chair, and he hobbled to the door with their help, of course.

Once inside Rooster admitted, "I thought I was a goner!"

He fell to the floor. "Get him some dry clothes," White Feather snapped. "I'll get him a shot of whiskey."

The men stood Rooster up and carried him to a chair. "Man, you must be crazy. What you's doing out in the weather like this?" another Indian asked.

Rooster responded, "Wudn't nearly this bad outside Templeton. Just as I got closer, the weather got worse."

White Feather remarked, "Been expecting you for the last week. Ms. Cadelia usually don't wait so long when she needs help."

"She's been busy, Deacon," Rooster explained. Rooster always called White Feather "Deacon." No one really knew why. He just called him Deacon for as long as one could remember.

Rooster screamed, "They at it again! They at it again! Yo' peoples done gotten angered up again."

White Feather nodded. "I've been feeling a bit weary for the last few weeks, but three days ago, I knew she was very disturbed.

"What we gotta do this time, Deacon? What we gotta do?" Rooster begged for an answer.

"Well..." White Feather said, scratching his head. "I presume her baby has been disturbed again. Why, when my people bury their dead, they don't want the spirits to be disturbed."

"Yes, sir, yes, sir," Rooster answered. "I understands that, but what we supposed to do now to satisfy that old Snow Princess?"

"Well, let me think a second or two," he asked. "Where did you find the baby skull?"

"To my understanding and my recollection..." Rooster explained. "Teddy Gail told me that Samantha found the skull in a trunk on the second floor."

"On the plantation?" White Feather asked for clarification. "Yes, sir, at Staunton Plantation on the second floor." Then he added, "What did she do with it?"

"Rosie told Samantha to carry it to Alligator Swamp and bury it near the water's edge."

Rooster answered.

"Did she do it?" White Feather asked.

"Naw," he remarked. "She grabbed the baby skull and hid it in the Negro's cabin under the bunk."

"Now let me think..." White Feather closed his eyes, then he said, "Rooster, you and the rest of the boys scat, so I can concentrate. She'll probably contact me and give me some instructions. Light the lanterns and close the door when you leave."

Rooster and the men went out the front door and stood around on the porch. The older Indian helped White Feather lay on the bed. He closed his eyes and began to mumble some sacred phrases.

"Jour la vouz, onza a, jour la vouz, shall a vouz, nil law law, zell law law."

Then he hesitated, and he repeated the chant two more

times. Then he laid back on the bed and slept.

Rooster and the other Indians came back into the cabin.

"Don't disturb him," one Indian said. "He is conversing with her. She is a very soft speaker, and he has to concentrate very hard to get the message."

"Well, what do we do now?" Rooster asked.

"He'll come out of the trance when he gets the message," the older Indian answered. "We'll just have to wait for him to wake up."

"The storm is almost over. Why don't you all go on the porch and play a game of checkers?" the older Indian suggested.

"And smoke a few weeds," another red man added.

The older Indian then added, "It shouldn't be too much longer."

The four Indians and Rooster went back out again to the front porch. Two men sat down at the table for checkers, and the other three men leaned against the post watching the rain. Two of the Indians lit their tobacco products, and one man pulled out a jug of whiskey cider, a concoction that White Feather sold to the customers when they had body ailments.

"What's wrong with you?" Kinko asked.

"Nuttin." Konko answered. "Just want to be prepared when my rheumatism starts acting up."

"Y'all are crazy," Rooster broke in. "Here, give me a swig of that tonic. When White Feather tells me what we gotta do to calm those Injuns, I'll need several jugs of the tonic."

The men waited another ten or fifteen minutes longer. Then White Feather began to holler for Rooster to come in. The five men went back into the cabin. Rooster went over to the bed, where White Feather had been lying. Rooster helped him sit on the bed.

"What did she say, what did she say?" Rooster begged for an explanation.

"The baby's skull has to be hidden securely in the grandfather clock. The grandfather clock is near the study at the end of the main hall. I don't know how long the baby skull has been in there, but somebody moved it. M. Shay is not going to let up until the baby skull is placed back in the secret compartment in the bottom drawer of the grandfather clock."

Stunned, Rooster asked, "Who is M. Shay?"

All the other Indians answered at once, "That's the Snow Princess."

"I never knew her name," Rooster admitted. "I just knew that when she got angry, all of us Negros tried to get her satisfied. Because you can't deal with these Redskins."

Then White Feather advised, "Rooster, then you know what you got to do."

"Yes, sir," he said with assurance. "Get the baby's skull back in the proper place."

"Be very careful, be very careful," White Feather warned Rooster. "Don't let anyone know what you are doing! Most folks do not understand Indian cultures or beliefs. Tradition says the infant skull will inhabit another body when he is born again on the right day and the right hour. That's why the old grandfather clock is so important. Because the clock is so programmed, and it keeps up with the exact hour that the skull will reappear. The clock knows the exact hour, place, and day of the new birth. And the Indians spirits are reunited within the new baby."

Rooster questioned, "How can the clock do all of that?"

"M. Shay's witchdoctor from her local tribe pro-grammed the clock when he set the baby's skull in the secret compartment.

"Oh," Rooster answered, and that's all he could say.

"My friend," White Feather then addressed Rooster. "You have a tremendous task to do. Don't mess up."

"Yes, sir, yes, sir." And with that, Rooster got back in his wagon and headed back to Staunton Plantation in Virginia.

As he was driving back to the plantation, he was thinking to himself, I always wondered why white folks cherished the old grandfather clock. Every time it stopped running, Mr. Staunton would call Mr. Caldwell in Boston Massa-chusetts to come spend the week with us to repair the old clock. I knew the clock was old. It came from somewhere across the ocean, and the family cherished it. I didn't know it had magical powers. I knew black folks believed in mag-ical powers. I guess white folks do too. We black folks don't tell white folks what we believe, so I guess white folks and red men don't tell what they believe either. Needless to say, I do have a big task to do, and best I get to it right now.

When Rooster finally made it back to Staunton Planta-tion, he went straight to Miss Cadelia.

"It's very simple, Miss Cadelia. All we have to do is put the baby's skull back into the secret compartment in the grandfather clock."

"Well, Rooster..." Miss Cadelia praised him. "That sounds simple enough. Be here tonight at twelve o'clock, quietly knock on my door, and we'll simply slip the baby's skull back into the old clock."

"Good enough, Miss Cadelia, I'll be here."

"Now, Rooster…" Miss Cadelia warned. "Don't you be sipping any moonshine before you show up. Any of your shenanigans, and this whole thing will blow up in our faces."

"Yes, ma'am," he replied, and he headed back to the bunkhouse.

Roddy met him at the end of the dirt drive. "Rooster, Mr. Staunton sent word for you to clean those four Appaloosas. He's got a buyer, and they'll be here in the morning to pick them up."

"Sure thing, Little Boss."

Rooster always called Roddy "Little Boss" because Carlton especially liked and trusted Roddy to get things done when he needed something concerning the plantation, the livestock, or the horses.

"Sure thing," he said again. But before I get started, Rooster thought to himself, I should stop in and check on Cotton.

Walking on down the road to the bunkhouse, he found Miss Josie standing outside the door.

"I need to see Cotton."

"Well…" Miss Josie muttered. "He's busy."

"Busy doing what?" Rooster demanded.

"Well, Ms. Tabitha is rubbing him down with some special ointment to relieve his injuries and speed up his healing process," she answered.

"Well, I need to see him."

Rooster pushed past Miss Josie and on into the bunkhouse. "Looks like he's healing pretty well if you ask me. I need to talk to you, Cotton. Right now."

Ms. Tabatha got up, put her clothes on, and quickly left

the cabin. She and Miss Josie made a quick departure and hastened toward the back field toward Templeton.

"Now what you doing messing up a good thing?" Cotton complained. "I ain't had none in over three weeks. I'm going to whip your ass myself."

Then Rooster told Cotton all about the visit to see White Feather and the instructions he had been given by White Feather.

CHAPTER 9

Red Man's Havoc

It was a quarter until twelve late that night, and you could hear two men running around in the bushes as they were sneaking up to the big house so as not to be heard.

"Shut up, Rooster, the whole house will hear you."

"Have you got the baby's skull?" Cotton shouted. "Have you got the baby's skull wrapped up? I sho' don't want the princess to think I've been messing with her baby boy. She'll be after me."

"Shut up, yeah, the skull is wrapped in a baby shawl from the last bout we had with those Injuns. Leddy Gail had it tucked away in the laundry chute. She knowed we'd probably be needing it again, and sho' nuff, time has come again."

When they got to the big house, Rooster tapped on Miss Cadelia's door. Miss Cadelia quietly opened the door and let the two men in.

"This way," she said, and the two men followed.

Miss Cadelia walked into the wide foyer in the middle of the house. The clock stood well over nine feet tall. It was a walnut and mahogany case with a molded cornice around the flat columns. Roman numerals surrounded the face of the clock with a silver ring enclosing a second reading and a date in the center, bearing a signature, "David Quare-London". At the bottom was a drawer, about seven or eight inches wide.

"There it is," Rooster exclaimed. "And there is the drawer we're supposed to put the Baby's skull in. Cotton and Miss Cadelia bent down, and Cotton handed this baby's skull to Miss Cadelia. He slowly opened the bottom drawer. When the drawer was opened, there were two compartments laying side by side. One compartment was opened, and the other was closed.

"Open both compartments," Miss Cadelia said.

"I can't open it!" Rooster replied. "Look, it takes a key to open this side."

Then Miss Cadelia bent down to look. "Okay, White Feather just said to lay this skull in the secret compartment, and we are through," Rooster said.

Then Miss Cadelia laid the baby's skull in the open compartment and quietly began to leave. Then the three of them got up to leave the grand hall. As they approached the door to leave, a loud cry was coming from the clock.

Startled, the three people looked around, and the cry of a baby got louder and louder.

"Quick!" Miss Cadelia said. "Get that skull before Mr. Staunton hears us and comes down."

The baby's cry got louder and stronger. Cotton ran to the clock, opened the drawer, grabbed the baby's skull, and Rooster and Cotton ran out the back door. They ran through the kitchen and out the back. They ran as fast as they could back into the woods behind the Negro quarters. The baby's skull was still hollering.

Miss Cadelia's bedroom was next to the kitchen. Miss Cadelia ran back to her bed, hopped in, and pretended to be asleep. All at once, they could hear Carlton coming down the stairs. He was in a hurry.

Lord, Miss Cadelia thought. I guess he was startled when he heard the scream, and he woke up. He must have heard all the commotion.

As Carlton stomped down the stairs, he was hollering to himself, "Miss Cadelia! Miss Cadelia! What did I hear? What is going on down here?"

Miss Cadelia quickly got up, threw the robe around herself, and tried to think of a good lie to tell Mr. Staunton. And, believe me, Miss Cadelia knew the lie needed to be a good one because he sounded furious!

When Carlton reached the bottom of the stairs, he entered the kitchen. Miss Cadelia was coming out of her bedroom door, as Carlton was entering the kitchen from the hall entrance.

"What was all that racket going all down here? I first thought I was dreaming, but the noise got louder and louder. Did you hear it, Cadelia?" Carlton demanded. "Did you hear all that commotion?"

Miss Cadelia was yawning and stretching like she had just woken up from sleep.

"I guess I'm used to it, Mr. Carlton," Miss Cadelia answered.

"Used to what?" he demanded again.

"Well, you know, old Sadie borned that baby calf last week," was Miss Cadelia's answer.

"Yeah, I remember," he replied.

"Well…" Cadelia added. "I can't for the life of me understand why she refused to let that little thing nurse, but for the last couple of nights, the boys have been bringing the little calf up, and Rosie has been bottlefeeding the little one. I guess, when she stops feeding, the little one goes to hollering. I guess he didn't get enough. So, Rosie would have to come back and mix up more formula, and I will agree that little calf does seem to know how to wake up the whole household."

"He sure does," Carlton answered. "You tell Rosie to take care of this matter before she goes to bed. I can't take any more of that crying."

"Yes," he added. "I thought for a minute that there was a baby crying in the house." Then he added, "It reminded me of the day Jessica Leigh was a baby."

"Yes, I remember," Miss Cadelia remarked.

"Miss Jessica would cry all night long. She had it bad with that old man, Mr. Colic. I sho' remember those nights here at the Staunton house. None of us's was worth a flitter the next day. I'll take care of this matter myself, and it won't happen again. I promise you that! It won't happen again."

"Goodnight, Miss Cadelia," Carlton said, and he went on to bed.

Cadelia sighed a breath of relief. She took off her robe, put on her gown, and got back into the bed. But believe me, Cadelia did not sleep one bit. All night long she wondered, what are we gonna do?

Just before daybreak, you could hear a rumble in the distance. Miss Cadelia opened her door, stepped outside, and looked toward Alligator Swamp. A grayish, white smoke was swirling from the old lagoon. The smoke got larger and larger. Miss Cadelia rubbed her eyes. She couldn't believe her eyes. She knew the Indians were well aware of what had happened in the past, and she was in terror about what they were planning this time. She quietly got out of the bed and tiptoed toward the corral. She made sure nobody saw her, but she knew she had better go see for herself just what was happening.

Old Jesse, the plowhouse mule, was sleeping next to the water trough. Miss Cadelia quietly woke her up and hitched her up to the wagon. Miss Cadelia knew she didn't have much time; daybreak would soon be upon her. Slowly, stirring old Jesse out of the barn, they rolled down the back road toward Alligator Swamp. The wind was blowing. The owls were hooting, and all the night varmints were scavenging and looking for food.

The old road came to end, and Miss Cadelia had to get out of the wagon and creep deeper into the lagoon toward Alligator Swamp. The cypress trees were covered with moss, and the thorns and heavy brush made it hard to walk down toward the lagoon area. The smoke was rising, and now she could smell the fire. As she crept closer, she could hear the Indian chants and the bones rattling. She gazed into the swamp. She caught a glance of the Indians. All she could see were white bones. It looked like twenty or thirty sets of bones coming out of the lagoon.

Each set popped up at four or five-minute intervals. Miss Cadelia knew at once they were doing a cloud dance. That was the talk among the Indians. When the Indian ancestors came out of the waters, they did the cloud dance. This dance would instruct the skies and clouds as to what damage the Indians wanted to be done. The cloud dance would also indicate to whom the interrogation was to be done. Usually, treacherous weather followed.

Miss Cadelia crept a little closer, and she saw what appeared to be the fur on a white bear. Beautiful, white peacock feathers, and white fur seemed to be floating in the air all by themselves. The rumbling bones danced around the white fur and peacock feathers. The bones would bow down, then they would jump up into the air. As the bones pointed toward the skies, the skies began to light up with the vibrant colors of the rainbow. The thunder began to roar and slowly the rain began to trickle down. Then the rain began to get heavier and at a steady pace.

Miss Cadelia was beginning to get wet, so she walked on back to the wagon. She got into the wagon and headed toward Staunton Plantation. By the time she got home, the sun was coming up, but the rain, still at a steady pace, was coming down. She walked in the back door, and Mr. Staunton met her.

"And where have you been so early in the morning?"

"Oh," she answered. "Just checking on that new calf."

"And how is he doing?" Carlton questioned her.

"Much better, much better," Miss Cadelia said. "He was nursing just fine. Old Sadie, the mama cow, must have finally decided to be a good mama and give the little thing her milk."

"Good," Mr. Staunton said. As he looked out the window, he remarked, "I didn't realize it was raining. Rain has not been predicted in the forecast for several weeks. However, I'm glad. I hope it lasts a few hours."

Huh, thought Miss Cadelia to herself. You hope it lasts

for a few hours. If I know those injuns, it will last for weeks--even months. It will last just as long as it takes to get that baby's skull back into the right shelf in the old grandfather clock.

Rosie and Miss Cadelia knew those Indians could cause droughts, tornadoes, and even flooding when they were upset with the white man. Rosie and Miss Cadelia knew what was happening; they just did not know what they were going to do.

The rain began to come. At first it was soft, sprinkling rain, then when the thunder roared, the lightning lit up the sky, and the rains began a steady pace, Rosie and Miss Cadelia knew it was not going to stop. Two days later, the rain had not stopped. It was not a strong, fierce rain, just a steady flow of precipitation with no signs of letting up. Miss Cadelia knew something needed to be done.

It was being discussed among the farmers and residents of Staunton. Questions were asked: "Where are the clouds coming from? How long will they last?"

Small creeks and gullies were filling up fast. The white folks wondered what was happening, and the black folks knew. They were all scared to death. Indian spirits are real, and the devastation they can cause can be crucial when the red man is disturbed by the white man's greed and destruction of their homeland.

Miss Cadelia had heard of violent storms, earthquakes, tornadoes, and even oceans running up onto dry land, drowning the town and victims themselves. Now Miss Cadelia and the other Negroes never admitted that all the bad weather was from Indian turmoil, but if the bad weather persisted, you had best be sending a message to the Native American spirits. Just be sure they are agitated or irritated because, as I said, the weather damage from Indian stress and agitation can be much more severe than the Indian massacres from the past.

Days three and four...

Pitter-patter of the rain. All eyes looking toward the sky. Shaking heads. Wondering, Why? Why won't the rain stop?

Miss Cadelia and the black folks knew that the Indian skull was the culprit. By now, all the blacks knew about the skull being placed in the grandfather clock. But the skull was not placed in the correct compartment in the clock. The secret drawer was locked, and Lord only knew Miss Cadelia did not have the key or have any idea where the key was. Two other times, Miss Cadelia, Cotton, and Rooster slipped into the house with the baby's skull. When they got to the grandfather clock, they tried again to get into the secret drawer, but each time they placed the baby's skull into the other drawer, the cry would begin, and the cry would not let up.

Finally, Miss Cadelia realized something.

"I've got to send Rooster back to town to share this information with White Feather."

Miss Cadelia thought, I'm sure he knows what's going on, and I have no choice.

The next morning, Rosie was stirring around in the kitchen.

"Go get Rooster and have him come to see me," Miss Cadelia told Rosie. "As soon as he gets through with his morning chores."

"Yes, ma'am," Rosie responded, and she murmured to

herself, "I hope he can get to White Feather before those Injuns get to us. I'm skaded, I'm skaded."

Rosie knew what had been done to Cotton, and she was scared to death. Rosie knew she had better not wander too far from Staunton Plantation. What had been done to Cotton could and would be done to her if she wandered around Alligator Swamp.

Then Rosie asked Miss Cadelia, "What's gonna happen? What's gonna happen now? I'm scared."

Miss Cadelia assured her, "We is doing the best we can do. All I can do now is send Rooster back to White Feather and relate the latest message. Hopefully, we can get this thing stopped before we all get flooded out of town."

Then Rosie inquired, "Miss Cadelia, why are the Red Men doing that to us any way?"

Miss Cadelia answered, "They are not angry at us colored folks, but they are mad at the white folks. When the white folks came, they stole the Indian lands, stole their heritage, and gave them nothing in return. The Indians living today can't do anything, but those Indian ancestors can cause havoc, if they are a mind to. So, Rosie..." Miss Cadelia instructed her. "Go get Rooster and send him to me. Hopefully, he can get on the road before dark."

"Yes, ma'am," Rosie replied, and she left to go get Rooster.

Rooster was in the wagon, heading toward Calhoun City. The rain was still pattering down – not heavy, but a steady rain. The same old Indians were sitting on the porch playing checkers and dipping snuff.

When Rooster walked through the front door of the trading post, White Feather remarked, "Been waiting on you, Deacon. Hoping it is not too late."

Then Rooster began to explain, "We did exactly what you told us to do. We wrapped the baby's skull inside a blanket and toted the baby's skull to the grandfather clock like you told us to do. That's where the problems began. There are two drawers on the bottom of the clock. One of the drawers was locked, so we tried to put the baby's skull in the drawer, which was not locked. We laid the baby's skull in the unlocked drawer, and we proceeded to leave the skull and go back into the kitchen. As soon as we left the room that dang baby skull let out a shrill cry like a baby hollering. The baby's skull screamed and screamed. The whole household was woken up. So, all we could do was pick up the baby's skull and blanket and get out of the house before Mr. Staunton caught us. We packed the baby's skull up and ran back into the woods behind the house."

"So, what happened then?" White Feather inquired.

Rooster continued his story. "Miss Cadelia made up some half-assed, wacky excuse, but the fact remains: the baby's skull ain't locked up in the secret drawer, and those Injuns are mad as hornets."

"Yes," White Feather agreed. "They are mad! M. Shay has been warning me for the last three days that she has had enough! Those Indian spirits got together down at Alligator Swamp. They formed the cloud dance, and the rains have begun."

"Will they ever stop?" Rooster asked pleadingly.

"Well," White Feather stuttered. "Only if M. Shay gets her request. That is, hopefully, before we all drown around these parts. I will guarantee you this, the rain will not stop until she is satisfied."

"But, but—" Rooster begged White Feather. "We do not

have the key to the drawer."

Then White Feather looked straight into Rooster's eyes and said, "An old Indian proverb says, 'look into the key-hole to see who holds the key.'"

"It's that simple?" Rooster asked White Feather surprisedly.

"Yes, it is," White Feather promised. "Just look into the keyhole to see who holds the key, then fetch the key and open the drawer and place the baby's skull back where it is supposed to be."

Then Rooster told White Feather goodbye and headed back toward Staunton Plantation with the new instructions. The rain was still pattering down with no sign of relief.

Early the next morning, Rooster headed toward the big house. He know that Miss Cadelia is anxiously awaiting to hear what White Feather had said concerning the baby's skull and its placement in the grandfather clock.

"Morning, Rooster," Miss Cadelia greeted him. "Figured you would be here bright and early."

"Yes, ma'am," he replied. "But the message he sends sounds rather strange to me."

"Sit down, Rooster," Miss Cadelia ordered. "Let me get you a cup of coffee, and you can explain all you can remember from White Feather's visit."

Miss Cadelia pulled out the kitchen chair. Rooster sat down, and Miss Cadelia poured him a cup of coffee.

"As best I can remember," he said. "M. Shay."

Miss Cadelia interrupted and asked, "Who is M. Shay?"

"That's the Indian princess; you knows, the mama of the baby skull boy," he explained.

"Oh, yeah, I remember," Miss Cadelia remarked.

Miss Cadelia remembered that night she was out at Alligator Swamp, when the Indians were doing the cloud rain dance praying and demanding that the rain continue to fall.

"Well, anyway," Rooster continued, "M. Shay has been warning White Feather for the last couple of weeks just what M. Shay expected us to do with the baby's skull. The rains are not going to stop until the baby's skull is placed back where it is supposed to be placed – on the bottom of the sacred shelf, at the bottom of the grandfather clock."

"We know that," Miss Cadelia sternly told Rooster. "But what did White Feather say about the key? We cannot unlock the locked shelf because we do not have a key to unlock the bottom shelf. One shelf is left open, and one shelf has to be unlocked with the key. The baby's skull clearly must go into the secret compartment, and we have to have a key."

Then Rooster explained, "White Feather said it is quite simple."

"Simple, hogwash!" Miss Cadelia exclaimed. "When you don't have a key, there's no way you can dream one up, and it will just appear, hogwash," Miss Cadelia said again in disgust.

Rooster continued, "White Feather said it's very simple. All you have to do is look into the key hole to see who holds the key. Then go fetch the key and unlock the bottom drawer."

"Rooster," Miss Cadelia vowed, "You must be loco. There ain't no way me or you or nobody our size can crunch ourselves little enough to see inside that keyhole. The keyhole is on the bottom part of the secret drawer. Neither I nor you can crunch our bodies down that far to see inside nothing, much less inside the keyhole."

Rooster interrupted, "Well, er, we just going to have to get some help."

"From who?" Miss Cadelia inquired.

"How about Junior?" Rooster answered.

Cadelia responded, "Junior, yes, Leddy Gail always fussin' at him. He loves crawling around on the floor of the cabin. Leddy Gail's always getting on to the boy for playing with the roaches.

Junior responded, "And his eyesight must be awfully good 'cause, Miss Cadelia, I swear I don't even see them roaches until Leddy Gail grabs 'em out his hand."

"Now, how old is he, Rooster?" Miss Cadelia asked.

"Well, let me see...he was born about the time..." He started counting on his fingers. "Remember when Cotton was a-courtin' Minnie Field Flowers, and they was a-swinging on Leddy Gail's wooden glider?"

Miss Cadelia said, "How old is Junior?"

"Well, don't you remember? When Minnie Fields broke her collarbone, she was laid up in the cabin house. Dr. Staunton came to see her, and it was that day when Lula Mae was giving birth to little Junior, about three years ago."

Then Miss Cadelia said, "Well, then, Rooster, Junior ought to be able to squeeze himself enough to peek inside that keyhole and tell us where the key is — what do you think?"

"Yes, ma'am," Rooster proudly answered. "Little Junior is as smart as a whip – just like his old dad."

"Huh," Miss Cadelia grunted. "Have him here tonight.

We will see how smart that boy is. Now be sure he don't cry. See y'all around midnight. Now get out of here, Rooster. I got my chores to finish up."

"Yes, Mamie," he responded. "I'll have Little Junior here by midnight, and he'll solve the problem once and for all."

As he was going out the door, his head was as big as a cantaloupe. He was so proud. Little Junior was a chip off the old block, and he'll be remembered for years to come for settling those Injuns down. Couldn't ask for a better hero. Little Junior, Rooster's only son, the cream of the crop on Staunton plantation.

Miss Cadelia knew time was passing by. She had worried for the past two hours, while

waiting on Rooster's response from White Feather. She knew Mr. Staunton and Aunt Martha would be down for breakfast.

"Rosie, Rosie," Miss Cadelia directed.

"Yes, ma'am," Rosie answered. "Set the table and go fetch Samantha. Tell her the floor needs to be swept, and the side steps need to be cleared off. Those old boxes that Helsinki drug up when Rooster brought the wheat flour in needs to be taken to the burn pit. Now, hurry. We runnin' late."

"Miss Cadelia, Miss Cadelia," Rosie interrupted. "What did Rooster say?"

"Rosie," Miss Cadelia answered. "I haven't got time to tell you. I've got to get this breakfast on the table. Oh, I hear them now."

Mr. Staunton and Aunt Martha were halfway down the stairs. Miss Cadelia ran to the hall door outside the kitchen, knowing she was very late for the breakfast. She had to make up something quick.

"Morning, Mr. Staunton," Miss Cadelia cheerfully said. "Miss Martha, I'm running a little late this morning. They must've had a ruckus in the hen house because it took quite a while to get the hens all settled down. Here, I've got your coffee made. Why don't you to just sit in the parlor for a spell, while I finish up your breakfast. I'll bring the coffee right in."

"That's fine," Mr. Staunton replied to Miss Cadelia. Then he turned to Martha. "Did you sleep well, sis?"

"Well, I think so, Carlton, except..." Aunt Martha replied. "Except..."

"Except what, sis?" Carlton inquired.

"Well, on and off, the whole night, I kept hearing something hit the window," Martha tried to explain. "I knew it wasn't hail, but it was so strange."

"Maybe..." Carlton responded. "It was a limb falling from that old oak tree next to your window. I told Cotton to cut it down. There were several dead limbs. I noticed them when that lightning storm hit the tree several months ago. I'll tell Cotton again."

"Carlton, you know I'm leaving for San Bernardino in two weeks. Jessica Leigh will soon be going to school."

"Yes." Carlton hugged Martha. "I'm sure going to miss you, but I know Josh has missed you tremendously."

Aunt Martha just smiled. "I do hope I have been some help."

"I'm sure you have," Carlton reassured her. "Jessica Leigh could never have made it without your help in calculus and physics. We just don't have qualified people to teach those classes in these parts. As a matter of fact, you would probably have to go to Charleston."

He hugged Martha. "Again, I love you, sis, and appreciate you so much."

"Oh, Carlton," Martha bragged. "I'm so proud of Jessica Leigh. If only Elizabeth could see her now."

"I'm sure she knows everything that's going on down here, and I'm sure she is proud of her also," Carlton replied.

"Breakfast is served," Miss Cadelia interrupted. "I might add it smells good. Just need two hungry folks to eat it up."

"Great!" Carlton said. "We're ready."

Meanwhile, back in the Negro cabins, all hell broke loose. Leddy Gail was ranting and raving. Tommy Toes was having a panic attack.

"What we gonna do?!" he asked. "What we gonna do?!"

Tommy Toes was a'clenching his hands together and wiping his forehead and repeating to himself, "What we gonna do?"

Rooster was trying to calm them all down, but it was too little too late, and Sylvester Rossetti was just a'rolling his eyes. Sylvester was the newest worker at Staunton Plantation, and he didn't know heads or tails of what was going on.

CHAPTER 10

Blackbird's Invasion

Mrs. Jessica Longmire from Longmire Plantation had already sent word that the blackbirds, hundreds of them, were falling out of the sky like falling stars, and Tabatha Wrongfellow said the fishes on her plantation were coming out of the rivers and walking on the land. Then they would swell up and pop open dead and the maggots was running loose everywhere. The black folks knew the Injuns were on the war path, and they wasn't about to let up. By noon, Staunton Plantation would be covered with black feathers and dry fish scales.

"But! But! But!" Rooster insisted. "We got the plan! We got the plan!"

"Shut up, you fool," Leddy Gail responded. "You ain't got no plan. I don't know what's worse, to drown in the flood like Noah's day or to be buried alive under dying blackbirds?"

"What we gonna do?!" Tommy Toes kept asking.

Leddy Gail knew by now that everybody on Staunton Plantation had heard about the Longmire Plantation and the Wrongfellow Plantation, and it was quite obvious that Staunton Plantation would probably be next.

Back in the big house, there was a knock at the door. Rosie went to open the door.

"It's Sheriff Crowder!" Rosie hollered to Miss Cadelia.

"Well," Miss Cadelia responded. "Ask the sheriff and his boys to come on into the kitchen."

"What's up, Mitch?" Carlton asked.

"Guess you heard," Mitch added.

"Heard what?" Carlton asked.

"Longmire Plantation is covered in dead blackbirds. Blackbirds are coming down from the north; must've gotten sick and lost their route," Sheriff Mitch explained.

"Lost their minds!" Jeremiah Sims butted in. "Lost their minds, if you ask me."

"How many of them?" Carlton interjected.

"Hundreds of them running into barns, flying into houses," Jeremiah said.

"What did Doc say?" Carlton asked.

"Couldn't find nothing wrong with them, just crazy."

"I suppose" was Sheriff Crowder's answer.

Then the sheriff added, "We hear tell a lot of fish from Wrongfellow Plantation are flooding up on shore, coming from all the rain we are having. Anyhow, we need as many men as you can spare to help clean up the mess, contaminated birds and contaminated fish. Can be awfully hazardous when you mix those poisonous fumes with all the rain, and we'll be run out of these here parts."

Carlton abruptly got up. "I got twenty five or thirty men. You can use all of them. We'll meet y'all at Canyon Tavern in a half an hour."

"Good," Jeremiah stated.

The sheriff and his men left and joined the rest of the

rescue mission.

Miss Cadelia stayed in the kitchen most of the afternoon, watching from her bedroom window. She could see in the distance, swarms of blackbirds, scouting the area, and looking for a place to dive and die. She also was watching the grandfather clock. It was 5:00 p.m. She didn't have to fix dinner that night, because Carlton and the men were still working on the cleanup. Lord, she hoped Little Junior could squinch his little body down low enough to see inside the keyhole that is our only hope.

The rain had picked up, and the winds were swirling in circular motions, kind of like tornado clouds. Only those who know the truth were terrified. The rest of the folks were just going through the motions. Everybody had gone to bed. It was 11:30 p.m., and Miss Cadelia kept looking out the kitchen door, waiting and watching for Rooster and Little Junior. Then she would walk back into the main hall and glanced at the old grandfather clock, and then worry a little bit more.

It was 11:40 p.m.

It was 11:45 p.m.

She went back through the kitchen and peep out the window.

"Well, it's about time."

She quietly opened the back door, made the motion with her hand using her index finger to shoo-shoo-shoo. Little Junior was a'rubbing his eyes. His t-shirt was all tattered and torn, and his long johns were way too big for him. He could hardly even walk because the long johns' fabric was dragging on the ground.

"Mamie," Rooster said. "I sho' hope this works. Hearsay

says there are twisters a'flying overhead near the east shore. I really don't know much about twisters, but I know plenty about Injuns, and the devilment they can cause."

"Quickly," Miss Cadelia said. "Get in here." Then she asked, "Rooster, are the birds still dropping?"

"Yes, ma'am, I see'd ten or fifteen new ones just a'coming from the cabins to the big house."

Then Miss Cadelia bent over and said to Little Junior, "Little man, we are counting on you."

"For what?" Little Junior answered. "Mamie, I can't do nothing. I'z too little."

Then Miss Cadelia said, "That's precisely why we need you…because you are just the right size."

Miss Cadelia put her arm around Junior and said, "Let me explain to you what we want you to do."

When she finished, he hollered, "I can do that, Mamie. I'z a big boy. I can do a little task like that."

"Shoo, shoo," Rooster instructed him. "Okay, let's get started."

Looking at the kitchen door and up the main stairway to the living quarters, Miss Cadelia felt it was probably pretty safe. The three tiptoed toward the grandfather clock. It was a pretty thing, so grand and stately. No telling how many secrets the old clock held. Nobody ever knew how old he was, but I'm sure if he would ever open up and talk, he would be pretty interesting because of all the history he had acquired over all the years.

As they were standing in front of the clock, the clock struck 12 a.m.

12 dongs.

Miss Cadelia thought to herself, I guess he talks every

hour, telling us the time of day.

Miss Cadelia asked, "See this drawer?" and pointed to the drawer with a keyhole.

The keyhole was about seven or eight inches from the bottom of the open shelf. That was the shelf they first put the baby's skull in. And we well remember the baby skull knew that wasn't where he was supposed to be going.

"Right here, Junior. Right here."

"I can see, Mamie," Junior replied. "I knows I'z to look inside the hole for a key."

Miss Cadelia instructed him again, "Junior, the key is not inside the hole, but you look inside the keyhole to see if you can see a key."

"Okay, Mamie." He bent down as far as he could bend. He tried several positions, but he couldn't get his eye positioned on the keyhole.

"I can't do it, Mamie!" Junior cried.

"Just as I expected. Okay, Junior, listen to me. Rooster is going to pick you up by your legs and turn you upside down," Miss Cadelia explained. "He's going to hold your head very close to the keyhole to see if you can see inside it."

Then Rooster picked Little Junior up, upside down, and placed his head close to the keyhole.

"Can you see anything?" Miss Cadelia asked. "Not yet. I can see inside the keyhole. It looks like a little room inside the keyhole. I see a bed and a slop jar."

Then Little Junior said, "I'm tired, turn me back up. My eyes are burning."

So, Rooster maneuvered him around and turned him right side up.

"What do we do now, Miss Cadelia?" Rooster asked.

"Let me go get Little Junior a glass of milk, and we will try again."

"I'd like some milk too," Rooster added.

Miss Cadelia went back into the kitchen, knowing that Little Junior was probably going to be on his head several times before he actually spotted the key. After swigging the milk, it was time to try again.

"You ready, Junior?" Rooster asked.

"I guess so," he answered. So, Rooster reached for the calves of his legs and picked him up again, as he inched him toward the keyhole again.

Junior started squirming. "You hurting my leg! You hurting my legs!" he exclaimed.

"Ease up on him," Miss Cadelia said. "You got him. He's okay. Just ease up on your squeeze."

After a minute or so, Miss Cadelia questioned Junior, "See anything? See anything?"

"Well, I still see the bed."

Miss Cadelia then told Junior, "We'll bend your head around to see what else you can see."

Then Little Junior exclaimed, "That's pretty! I can see that pretty glass that shines from the second-floor window. We love staring at the colored glass. It shines so pretty in the sunlight."

"Oh! Oh!" Little Junior screamed, "Let me squint my little eyes. I can see, I can see it. Looks like an angel."

Then he started complaining. "My head is hurting again. I gotta get my head up right. Turn me over."

Miss Cadelia told Rooster to put him right side up.

Then Little Junior added, "Do I get some more milk?"

"Yes, in a minute."

"Rooster," Miss Cadelia said. "There is an angel built in the crown molding right above the stained-glass window. I always have to get Helsinki to bring up the ladder when I clean the glass. I do it every couple of years."

"How about my milk? I want my milk," Junior demanded.

"Shut up, Junior. Miss Cadelia is going to get it for you in a minute."

Then Rooster said to Miss Cadelia, "Did you ever see the key when you was on the ladder?"

"No," Miss Cadelia responded. "Why would I? I was never looking for a key. Why would anybody put a key where you couldn't see it or reach it?"

"I don't know," Rooster answered, puzzled.

"Let me go get Junior's milk."

She went back into the kitchen, got him a cup of milk, and brought it to him. Junior was rolling around on the floor, enjoying the thick rug in front of the old grandfather clock.

"Drink the milk Junior," Miss Cadelia said. So, Junior sat up and drank the cup of milk.

"Ready to try again Miss Cadelia?" Rooster asked.

"I guess so," Miss Cadelia responded, instructing, "Tell him to look around the angel. Look around her head and look around her arms, her dress…just look all around the angel figure."

"Okay, Mamie."

With his eyes glued on the keyhole, Junior started hollering, "I see it! I see it! I see it!"

"What do you see, Junior?" Miss Cadelia questioned.

"A key," he answered. "She has the key around her neck.

It's gold, and it looks like an X, only it looks like a crooked X."

"Then it must be a cross," Miss Cadelia said. "A crooked X would look like a cross."

"Now, look again, Junior, to be sure," Miss Cadelia ordered him.

"I'm sure enough, Mamie, I see it," Junior snapped back. "A pretty gold necklace that has an X on the end of it."

"Okay, Rooster. Turn him right side up," Miss Cadelia exclaimed. "White Feather was right. How that key got on top of that stained-glass window, I swear I have no idea. But that's what we gotta do. Some way or another, we gotta get the key off her neck to unlock the secret compartment."

"Do I get more milk? Do I get more milk?" Junior argued.

"No, child, Rooster needs to get you back to bed."

Then Miss Cadelia bent down, hugged Little Junior, and said, "Son, you have been a blessing. Now you and Rooster head on back to the cabin. I'm sending you a batch of rolls, just for you two for the good work y'all have done."

"Thanks, Mamie," he replied.

The two proudly tiptoed back through the kitchen, picking up the sack of rolls and heading back to the Negro quarters. As Rooster and Little Junior headed out the back door, down toward the cabins, they were shocked. Blackbirds were everywhere. They hadn't been making any noise while Little Junior was looking inside the keyhole, but they were all sitting real still on the fence posts, all lined up behind the big house. The birds were staring toward Rooster and Little Junior.

As they took a few steps, the birds began to shutter

around a bit. When Rooster and Junior stopped walking, the birds would get still again.

"What we gonna do?" Little Junior asked.

Rooster responded, "We gonna run like wildfire, and I hope we get to the house before they get us."

Then Rooster and Junior began running toward the Negro quarters. It was very strange. The birds did not move one inch. Rooster was running as fast as his long legs would carry him. He even stopped and picked up Little Junior, and they ran on to the Negro quarters. It must've been around 12:30 a.m. because every half hour the old grandfather clock would chime in a simple tune that kind of sounded like you were playing the scales on the piano.

As the night progressed, the chimes would get an octave lower. Miss Cadelia went on back to bed very satisfied, feeling sure the mystery had been solved. Once she got the key off the angel, all the problems would be solved. She took her robe off and got into bed. Sleeping pretty soundly, Miss Cadelia was finally in a deep sleep. Lord only knew she needed it. The problem of putting the baby skull back into the locked drawer had been a puzzle to everyone and a big worry to all the residents of Staunton Plantation. Miss Cadelia was finally satisfied that everything was going to be okay.

All at once, Miss Cadelia was startled. She sat up in bed, rubbed her eyes, and thought, "What in the hell is happening?"

Putting on her robe, she ran through the kitchen to the hall door, facing the winding staircase. Mr. Staunton, Aunt Martha, Teddy Staunton, and Leslie Tatum were running down the stairway in panic.

"Get the shotgun." Carlton told Teddy it was in the hall closet. "Leslie, you and Aunt Martha use the twelve-gauge. That will be easier to handle."

Miss Cadelia was shocked with panic. "What is happening? What is happening?" she screamed.

"Haven't got time to talk, Miss Cadelia. Gunfire's coming from the lagoon. Several windows are broken out on the second floor, and the stained-glass window is shattered to pieces. Must have been a lot of outlaws 'cause every few minutes you could hear the bullets hitting the house."

"How many do you think we're fighting?" Miss Cadelia questioned. "No idea, but by the gunshots, must be a dozen or so," he answered.

Carlton rushed out the side kitchen door, and Teddy headed out the front hall, off the front porch. Leslie and Aunt Martha took to the west of the house with guns pointing at each window. When they got outside, all the colored folks had congregated up towards the big house. Blackbirds were flying everywhere. They were flying into the glass panels of the windows. Rooster and Little Junior were holding each other tight.

"Well, I'll be damned," Carlton said. "There were no outlaws, just those dang blackbirds, flying into the window panels of the house. The force was so strong that they would fall dead upon impact. I guess they broke their necks."

Carlton fired several shots, and Teddy did the same thing. They were in the front yard, and the remaining birds scattered and flew back toward the lagoon. Leslie and Aunt Martha came outside.

Leslie said, "We figured Staunton Plantation would be

next on the blackbird route, didn't we?"

"Yes, but I didn't figure on this much damage."

Walking around the back of the house, they discovered all the windows had been shattered; all the paint had been scraped off the wood, and hundreds of holes had been pierced into the frame house. There were hundreds of dead birds lying on the ground.

"When is this ever going to stop?" Leslie questioned. "When is this ever going to stop?"

"I don't know," Carlton answered. "All the colored folks are rumoring that this is a curse of the Cherokees."

"What do you mean?" Leslie questioned.

"Well, you know, I don't believe half of what those Negroes say, but they firmly believe that dangerous weather conditions are related to the angry moods of the Indian spirits in Alligator Swamp," Carlton tried to explain.

"What?" Leslie looked puzzled.

"Well," Carlton continued. "Alligator Swamp used to be an old Indian burial ground. Hearsay is that when those spirits get mad or angry, they take it out on the settlers living in the area."

"Mad about what?" Aunt Martha asked. "What could they be mad about?"

"I don't know," Carlton responded. "I really don't know. The coloreds won't talk. They think differently from us white folks, and they firmly believe that Indian spirits still prevail on the earth around these parts and cause havoc when necessary."

Leslie was very puzzled. She has never heard anything so absurd. She remarked, "I can't believe, Martha, I can't believe any of this nonsense."

"Oh well," Carlton continued. "I'm just telling you what I've heard from the past. Just bits and pieces of weird happenings from old Indian customs."

Then Carlton and Teddy walked toward the ladies.

"Let's go on back in," Carlton ordered. "I told the hired help to go on back to the cabins, and we would clean up this mess tomorrow."

Carlton looked at Aunt Martha, and Martha asked him, "What do you really believe is happening around here?"

"I have several suspicions, but I can't swear about anything. Try not to worry, Martha. You'll be leaving Staunton soon. I'm sure Josh will be glad to have you home," he advised her.

"Yes, he's wired me twice today. He is anxious for me to come home."

Then Carlton put his arm around Leslie. "Are you, all right?" he asked.

She smiled and responded, "Yes, Carlton."

"I've just never heard of anything like this," Carlton said. "Don't be frightened. I'm sure it will all be over soon."

"I'm glad the children are not here," Teddy said.

"Me too," Carlton replied. "It was nice of Mrs. Higginbotham to invite them over to spend the night. The children enjoyed the church social, so Mrs. Higginbotham invited some of the children over for the night. Couldn't have been better timing."

"You are right. This incident would have frightened the daylights out of them. They are scared to leave the house like it is with the talk and all," Teddy added.

Then all four of them walked back inside the house, up the stairs, and went on back to bed. Everybody was now back in their bedrooms. Cardboard and wood pieces had been placed over most of the broken windows, and everybody was back in bed, hoping to get a few hours of sleep. Miss Cadelia was back in her bed. Just as she was beginning to ease off to sleep, she heard pecking on the window. She knew it wasn't a bird, because they always flew like a raging bull, as they plundered into the windows. Looking out the window, she motioned for Rooster to come to the back-kitchen door.

Then Miss Cadelia scolded him, "What you want, Rooster? It ain't but an hour or so before daybreak."

"Mamie, Mamie, I knows I ain't the smartest Negro on the plantation...maybe I is the coolest, but I knows I ain't the smartest," he tried to explain.

"What you driving at, Rooster?" she snapped at him.

"Well, Mamie," he continued. "Just supposing the black-birds was looking for something."

"Looking for what, you crazy fool?!" Miss Cadelia exclaimed.

"A key, maybe," he murmured.

Miss Cadelia stopped quickly in her tracks, dumbfounded. "Rooster!" she exclaimed. "You could be right. Those dang birds ransacked the Longmire Plantation! They tore up the whole Wrongfellow Place, and now they are after us."

Then Rooster announced, "Why don't you tiptoe up to the second floor and check the Angel?"

"Rooster," Miss Cadelia said. "You can't see no angel at night, much less a key around her neck. I'll have to wait 'til morning."

"Morning may be too late," he tried to explain. "If the

Angel and key fell when the stained-glass was shattered, they'll just clean it all up as rubbish. Nobody will notice that old key."

Miss Cadelia hesitated again, "Let me think a minute. By daylight, Leslie, Aunt Martha, Carlton, and Teddy – hell, all of them will be inspecting these rooms on the second floor."

"Then it will be too late! Think fast, Mamie. The clock is ticking," he reminded her. "Think fast."

She concluded, "You are right! You are so right!"

Then Miss Cadelia lit the kerosene lantern, and the two of them proceeded up to the second floor directly to the baby's room. Little Jesse was born fourteen years before; as a matter of fact, it was fourteen years to this very day. They finally got up the long, winding staircase. Low and behold, there were several dead birds in the hallway, and when they got to the room with the stained-glass window, there were more than a half a dozen more birds, some still alive as they lay dying, moaning like sounds of death.

"Here, let me see the lantern," Rooster said, and he took the lamp from Miss Cadelia. They stepped over the birds and got near the window. Three-fourths of the window had been shattered and had fallen to the floor.

When they used the lantern to see the floor, Miss Cadelia exclaimed, "There she is – the Angel."

She was about six or seven inches tall. She looked like she was made from carved mahogany. She had doubled-arched, scrolled, carved wings on each side of her shoulder.

"One arm must have been broken from the fall," Miss Cadelia remarked. "Because here is the other missing piece."

"But where is the key?" Rooster said. "I don't know. Let's keep looking."

For the next fifteen or twenty minutes, Miss Cadelia and Rooster combed through the room, piece by piece.

"It's not here. It's not here. Maybe Little Junior was wrong. Maybe he just imagined he saw a key," Rooster fretted.

"No," Miss Cadelia responded. "He saw one, and I bet my money on a bale of hay one of the blackbirds got it."

"Why, what for?" Rooster questioned.

"I don't know, I simply don't know" was the only answer Miss Cadelia had.

Looking out the window, Miss Cadelia could barely see the sun coming up over the eastern horizon.

"We gotta go," she abruptly snapped. "They'll be up soon."

"Okay," Rooster said disappointedly. "I guess."

"You guess what, Rooster!" Miss Cadelia announced as she went down the stairs. "You can't guess nothing. All we know is that the key is not on the Angel, and the key is not in this room. So, we are back to square one. Let me go on down and get ready for breakfast."

The rains were still coming down. Twisters were predicted all over the Mideast, and warnings of snow and hail were in the forecast. All Miss Cadelia could do was shake her head. She simply did not know what to do.

Aunt Martha had recently returned from Wilshire Academy in New Hampshire. Jessica Leigh had just been accepted to the elite academy. Her mother finished at this academy, and, although her mom was dead, everyone in the Staunton household knew Jessica Leigh would follow in her footsteps. During the pioneer days, this family enjoyed eating together and having political and business discussions around the kitchen table or dining table. Doctor Staunton was getting prepared to go to Washington for a political meeting. Both of the Staunton brothers were bureaucrats, very influential in assisting the president in running Congress. At this period of time, tobacco plantations and tariffs concerning embargoes were very conservative. The brothers represented the tobacco plantation farmers quite well.

Agnes, George, and Cousin Sabrina were spending the week at Staunton Plantation, while their father is in Washington. Since Doctor Staunton was the local physician in Templeton, Virginia, he was a very influential person. Carlton Staunton was at the kitchen table, reading something in a magazine or brochure from the local seed and feed store. The three children were seated around the table. Miss Cadelia had just prepared the meal and was beginning to set the food on the table.

"Miss Cadelia," asked Mister Staunton. "Are you going to call your sister?"

Mr. Carlton replied, "No. She's awfully tired from the long trip back from Wilshire Academy. I just told her to rest, and we would to take her supper up."

Miss Cadelia then reminded the children, "Eat up! We've got lots to do before bedtime. I've got to check over that homework, and we've got to scrub some of that Virginia dirt from behind your ears."

Then Sabrina piped in. "I ain't dirty. I don't need no scrubbing."

George then looked at Sabrina and pointed his finger. "Papa said you had to bathe, and you know he told me to report everything back to him that was uncalled for."

"Don't worry, Uncle Carlton," Agnes said, as she was warning George. "I'll take care of Sabrina. She won't give you a speck of trouble. We made a pact before Paw left, but now tattletale George may be another matter."

Miss Cadelia said, "I've already fixed a tray of food, Aunt Martha. Let me give it to you, and you can carry it up."

"Thanks," Mr. Carlton replied, and he carried the big old wooden tray upstairs. First, he washed his hands. He did not know why, but he had a habit of washing his hands before and after meals. As Carlton was starting up the stairway, two ranch hands rushed in. They were hollering and screaming. They were young men. The young ranch hands are very hard-headed. Sometimes they thought they knew a lot about everything and had a tendency to cut corners.

Carlton gave instructions to Cotton. Cotton, in return, was to relay the message to the young ranch hands. The young ranch hands, many times, thought their way was better, but Mr. Carlton was very patient and understanding. He always treated the boys like they were his own sons. Miss Cadelia had seen it over and over again, but after the young ranch hands had had a few hard knocks, they finally began to listen.

Mr. Carlton looked around and calmly said, "What's wrong, boys?"

Both boys were stuttering and stammering, so much that Mr. Carlton could make no sense of what they were trying to say.

"The Appaloosas...the Appaloosas are out!"

"What?!" Mr. Carlton hollered.

Then Montana spoke up. "We were checking the fences in the West field. The twister damaged over three quarters of an acre last week. Cotton told us to check it out."

Josh then spoke up. "Christago moved the herd to the east field, but he must've moved them back 'cause there ain't no sign of no horses in the left or right field."

"Where are they?" Carlton asked.

"We didn't do nothing wrong, did we?" Josh questioned.

"Did you all repair the fences?" Carlton asked.

Montana responded, "Well, er—not yet. That's what we were doing today, when we got sidetracked."

Mr. Carlton then spoke up rather sternly. "Rex and I moved the herd on to the next county when you all failed to fix those fences. Rex had to detour the herd in the opposite direction. I was wondering when you all would discover them missing!"

"Well, er, well, er..." Josh stammered.

"I thought—" Montana spoke up.

"You didn't think at all. I knew we should have listened to Cotton instead of waiting for all those boys from Rusty Creek.

"They took the cider whiskey."

Hearing that, Mr. Carlton said, "What did you say?"

Montana quickly responded, saying, "Oh, nothing, Mr. Carlton, oh nothing. I'm awfully sorry. It won't happen again. Come on, Josh."

As they walked out the door, she said, "We got work to do. We got to figure out a way to get our money back. We were hijacked out of ten dollars and a jug of whiskey. We must be fools."

The two walked out toward the bunkhouse. Mr. Carlton just shook his head and walked on up the stairs. When he got to Aunt Martha's room, he knocked on the door.

"Come on in, Carlton," said Aunt Martha. She recognized the walk. He walked in and set the tray down on the end table next to the bed.

Carlton bent over toward her and whispered, "Feeling better, sis?"

Martha answered, "Much better. That train ride just about did me in."

"How is Jessica Leigh?" Carlton asked.

"Oh, she will be fine, Carlton. The Academy is so nice. I now know why you wanted her to attend. She'll do fine, Carlton. I do not believe she won't be coming home until Thanksgiving. Doctor McKinley – Alexander – said the freshmen usually stay at least four months before they are allowed to come home. Policy and rules. So many girls get homesick, and they say they adjust better if they stay the full four months for the registration and period of adjustment."

Mr. Carlton could tell Aunt Martha was awfully tired, plus the fact that in a couple of days she would be on another journey back to California.

"I'll leave you be."

He kissed Martha's forehead. "Your food is getting cold," he commented.

Then he walked out of the room and down the stairs. Martha put her hand in her coat pocket and gaped at the ruby cufflink she pulled out of her pocket. By the smile on her face, you could see she had pleasant memories – memories that were associated with the ruby cufflink.

The next morning, Carlton said, "The train will be leaving at 1 p.m. this evening. You got all the bags packed?"

"Yes, Carlton, Josh is so ready for me to be back in California."

Then she remarked, "Breakfast smells good! Let's see what Miss Cadelia has cooked for us this morning."

"Come on in! Good morning," Miss Cadelia said to Martha and Carlton. "Where is Miss Leslie?"

"She's on the way down," Carlton replied. "Okay, by the way, Teddy left early this morning. He had a patient to see in Calhoun City. He knew he wouldn't have time for breakfast."

"Okay," Miss Cadelia replied, and she began to serve breakfast.

"You all have a lot of work to do today," Martha exclaimed.

"Yes," Miss Cadelia replied. "Clean up this place from the blackbird invasion."

"Carlton," Martha spoke again. "I hate to leave you all at this time with so much work to do, bad weather and all."

"Don't worry about it, Martha," Carlton interjected. "We've had bad and unpredictable weather before."

All Miss Cadelia could do was roll her eyes and think to herself, But you ain't never had nothing like this and it ain't over yet!

They began to eat the delicious breakfast.

"Mr. Carlton," Miss Cadelia said.

"Yes, Miss Cadelia?" he replied.

"You remember Lucy Jo Ratliff?"

"Yes, I do recollect meeting her once," he remembered.

"Yes, she works for the Townsend family near Oak Grove."

"Well, er, she's been having a lot of personal problems. Her boys done run away, and she's got bad rheumatism. She sent word that she would like to see me, if it's all right with you. I was going to take the wagon and try to see her sometime this morning. I'll be back by noon," she assured him.

"Take your time, Miss Cadelia. Take your time," Carlton agreed.

Carlton turned to Martha, and he hugged her really tightly. Tears were streaming down her face, and Martha said, "I'm going to miss y'all. I have enjoyed my time here and at Wilshire Academy with Jessica Lee. Jessie is doing so good at school."

"It's been so good having you here with us," Carlton addressed her. "We all love you. When you're here, everything just seems perfect, Martha."

Martha assured him, "And I'll certainly miss you all."

"I'll be taking you into town around 12 o' clock. The train leaves at 1 p.m.," Carlton noted.

Then Carlton added, "I know Josh is eager to have you home."

"Yes, he is. It's been a long five months, but he is very cooperative because he knows little Jessica needed my assistance, and it does seem like the tutoring paid off. Her first term grades were very good."

"So, Mr. Carlton," Miss Cadelia interrupted. "I'm going to finish up the dishes and go on into town."

"Fine, and, Miss Cadelia, take your time. You get out so very little. Just take your time and tell Lucy Jo hello,"

Carlton replied, "I will."

Miss Cadelia went back to doing the morning dishes.

As quickly as she could finish washing up the dishes and putting up the pots and pans, she was concentrating on one thing.

"I've got to get to White Feather."

Going to the closet, she picked up the rain wrap and umbrella. Looking out the window, she spotted Sylvester and Rosetti. They were near the barn. They were picking up the dead birds and taking them to the fire pit.

"Sylvester, Sylvester," she hollered. "Quick, hitch up the wagon and put on the cover. I've got to go to town."

"Yes, ma'am," he responded. "It must be pretty important for you to be out so early in the morning."

"It is. Believe me, it is," she replied.

Miss Cadelia got into the wagon and headed toward Calhoun City outside Templeton, Virginia. The winds continued to blow. Twister-like gusts of wind swirled around and around. The rains had let up a bit, but the trickling few drops formed a fine mist, as Miss Cadelia held the reins and use the whip to hurry old Jessie along. Jessie was Miss Cadelia's personal horse. She had owned him ever since he was born.

"Hurry, boy, hurry, boy!" she screamed. She used the whip harder. She knew she needed to get to White Feather and give him the latest information. Things were really getting out of hand. Miss Cadelia knew she had to speak to White Feather herself.

As she neared town, she could see the Indian trading post. Oddly enough, White Feather

was sitting on the front porch. He was seated in his old cowhide rocker, as though he was expecting her.

"Figured you'd be here," White Feather said."

"White Feather," Miss Cadelia questioned. "You got the key, don't you?"

He stuck his old, rough and scarred hand into his pocket. He pulled out the key and handed it to her.

"You'd best be on your way, Miss Cadelia, and hurry," he suggested. "M. Shay is about to erupt, and it'll be too late to turn back time."

Miss Cadelia took the key and motioned with her hand a thank you, then returned to the wagon. She headed back to Staunton, Virginia. Miss Cadelia was so very thankful to be holding the key in her hand. She held it in the palm of her hand. It did look like an X. When you turned it right side up, it was a cross, a very old sculptured cross. Each of the four ends of the cross had two arms that extended right below the ends, so it didn't matter which way you turned it. The cross was always obvious. Each of the four ends had an X engraved into the metal. Three small stones that looked like glistening diamonds were on each end. So, altogether, there were twelve bright and shiny particles that looked like diamonds.

Miss Cadelia had always heard about the pirate treasures coming to the New World, and diamonds, rubies, jewels, sapphires, and all the expensive stones that the pirates had stolen from the cargoes, while sailing on the high seas. Miss Cadelia squeezed the key in her hand. It must have had magical powers because she could feel the tingling in her hand. She also felt a surge of strength, as she carried the metal cross key in her hand. I must go home quickly. White Feather gave warning that M. Shay was angered, and her destruction could become worldwide.

Carlton met Miss Cadelia, as she and old Jessie rolled

down the road to the main house.

"Did you get Lucy Jo's problems worked out?" Carlton asked.

Miss Cadelia looked puzzled, then she remembered the lies she had told to Mr. Staunton.

"Oh, yes, oh, yes. I do believe just being with her gave her a chance to air her feelings, and she'll be better able to deal with her situation," Miss Cadelia answered. Then she questioned, "Did Aunt Martha get off okay?"

"Yes, the train was 30 minutes late due to the bad weather up north," Carlton explained. "But she got off and was quite eager. She's been away from Josh for a long time. As a matter of fact, I don't believe she's ever been away from him for this many months at a time."

Then Miss Cadelia interjected. "Hope she has a good trip home."

"I do, too," Carlton replied.

Miss Cadelia remarked, "The grounds look pretty good."

"Yes, the boys spent all afternoon picking up the rubbish."

"Cotton started the fire on the north end, and they burned all the birds and all the loose feathers. I hope this will be the end of the bird invasions."

Miss Cadelia thought to herself, It will be the end if and only if I get that skull back in the grandfather clock.

Then Carlton walked on toward the stables, and Miss Cadelia came on back toward the house. Before she could get into the house, Rosie and Samantha met her at the door. Looking around for Mr. Staunton, the two knew he was heading toward the stables.

They both hollered at the same time, "Did you get the key?"

"Quiet! You two gals know to be careful in this house," Miss Cadelia snapped. "You can never be too careful! You don't know who is a'coming around the corner. You know walls can talk."

"Yes, Mamie, but did you get the key to the drawer?" they kept asking.

"Yes." She opened up her hand. "Let me hold it! Let me hold it." Samantha begged.

Miss Cadelia allowed her to hold the key, but only for a few seconds.

Now Miss Cadelia suggested, "Now, you gals get on back to your chores. I knows y'all ain't done nothing while I was gone."

"Yeah," Samantha told Rosie. "I told you to hang out those clothes in the barn, and now you wait 'til afternoon."

Samantha took the basket of wet clothes and headed for the clothesline.

Then Rosie said, "When you gonna put it back in the drawer?"

"Probably tonight after everyone's in bed," Miss Cadelia responded. "Go tell Leddy Gail, I'll be down sometime after dark and have the skull ready, 'cause I'm anxious to get that thing back in its rightful place."

"Me too," Rosie replied. "Me too."

The rain was still coming down. Twisters were rumored all over the county. Hail and rain were dropping all over the Mideast. Miss Cadelia was nervously working in the kitchen. She was simply waiting on the family to go to bed, so she could go down to the Negro quarters and get the skull.

The clock struck 10, then 10:30. She came out of the

kitchen door, looked up the stairway to the second floor. Carlton's lantern was still on. Miss Cadelia paced back and forth, back and forth. She was holding the key in her hand. She was just wanting the whole ordeal to be over.

Finally, after she looked up the stairway seven times, the light had gone out.

Good, she thought. Now I can get this done. I can get that darn skull in the clock.

She threw on her rain wrap and went out the back door. She saw the kerosene lanterns still burning in the Negro quarters. She knew they were waiting on her to get the skull. When she finally arrived at the cabin, she knocked on the door. Leddy Gail quietly opened the door.

"It's about time. I didn't know when you was coming."

"Carlton just blew out his light," Miss Cadelia explained.

Then Leddy Gail motioned for Rosie, and Rosie brought the tiny skull, wrapped in a bearskin hide.

Good, thought Miss Cadelia. This bearskin will be offered as an apology for the removal of the skull.

Several strands of Indian beads were intertwined in the skull and hide.

"Please be careful," Rosie said. "Please be careful."

Miss Cadelia carefully took the baby skull wrapped in the bear hide and tucked it inside her wrap and headed toward the big house. She could hardly walk, with the circular motions of the winds. Quickly, she made her way back to the back door.

The rain was coming down: pitter, patter, pitter, patter, pitter, patter.

Once inside the house, she gave a sigh of relief. She went to the door, looking up the stairway. She looked down at the skull, remembering the last time she tried to put it in the drawer.

"Please, dear Lord, let this work." She closed her eyes and whispered a prayer.

Then, she quietly went toward the grandfather clock, and, using the cross-shaped key, she opened the secret compartment of the clock. Slowly, the key turned, and the door opened. Miss Cadelia gently put the bear hide and the baby skull into the secret compartment.

She then locked the drawer back and returned to the bedroom. She waited and waited and waited. Undoubtedly, the Indian princess, M. Shay, was satisfied because the rain stopped instantly and the twisters vanished. Miss Cadelia looked out the window, and the sky was clear, and there was no rain or wind.

"Thank you, Lord," Miss Cadelia said, expressing her gratitude. Her task was complete, and she went on back to bed, still holding the key in her hand.

CHAPTER 11

Wilshire Academy

Jessica Leigh was sitting on the bed writing a letter to Sabrina.

Dear Sabrina,

Things are okay, but believe me, Wilshire Academy is not as great as Daddy and Uncle Teddy described. I have three roommates. Two snooty and snobby ones, and one plain Jane. I think I like plain Jane the best. Her name is Hortense Crowder, and she is an all-around bookworm. She hangs out in the library all afternoon. She belongs to the chess club and attends seminars on Plato and Aristotle at night. She goes to bed at 9 p.m. sharp. She wears blinders on her eyes and wears earphones so she can sleep without disturbance. But the other two girls, Mary Margaret Alexander Ford and Elizabeth Roshavick, are simply sickening and disgusting.

We have swim classes twice a week, and Mary Margaret is so frightened of the water. She sits on the side of the pool and dangles her feet in the shallow end. Then Elizabeth is always sick or either she pretends to be sick. Always on Tuesday and Thursday, she has a stomach virus or headache or she didn't sleep well. Anyway, when it comes to sports, these two girls are sticks in the mud. The food is okay – nothing like Miss Cadelia's home cooking. But I'll make it. Well, guess I better go. The two snobs are in ballet class, and they will be returning before long. I want to get my clothes folded before Madeline, the hall monitor, comes in for room check. Madeline is a snooty person, too. She loves to report us when the room is not up to her specifications.

Gotta go,
Jessica Leigh

Back in Crimson Hall, the ballet classes were going on. Sister Athea Stettson was the dancing instructor. She was in her mid-30's and a graduate of Wilshire Academy – a very attractive and distinguished lady, but very firm. There were girls in the ballet class ranging from twelve to sixteen years of age.

"Mary Margaret," Sister Athea Stettson reprimanded. "You are not paying attention. Your timing is off-balance, and your posture is intolerable. So please concentrate on what you are doing."

Mary Margaret nodded her head and got back in step. The music played on, and when the music stopped, Sister Athea Stettson said, "Okay, girls, for the remainder of the session, we will spend time on the bar doing our stretches."

The next day, Hortense and Jessica Leigh were walking

to the main hall on campus. This was the math department, where calculus, physics, trigonometry, and advanced trigonometry were taught. As they turned and headed toward the building, an elderly man approached them.

"Well, hello, Dr. McKinley," Jessica Leigh greeted him.

Dr. McKinley peered down from his wire-rimmed glasses and said, "Oh, hello, Miss Staunton. How are things going with you?"

"Fine – just fine," she responded. "The classes are okay, but I'm having a hard time familiarizing myself with the location of the buildings on campus. Why, I am running myself from one end of the campus to the other. Maybe once I learn my way around, it won't be so confusing."

Then Dr. McKinley looked at Jessica Leigh and said, "I really enjoyed meeting your Aunt Martha. She is a very interesting person. Has she gone back to California yet?"

"Yes," Jessica answered. "She returned to Staunton Plantation and stayed a few days and then went back to California."

Then Jessica added, "Her husband is much older than she is, and his health worsened while she was out here, so she felt the need to go back home."

"How is he doing? I mean her husband, how is he doing now?" Dr. McKinley asked.

"Not much better as of last report, but thanks for asking. I'll tell Aunt Martha you were asking about her husband," Jessica added.

"Oh, yes," Dr. McKinley replied. "Tell her I was concerned. Well, I must be going. I have a conference in Hand Hall, and I'm sure you girls need to be going to class."

As the girls entered the classroom, several students

gathered around them.

"Have you heard? Have you heard!?" the students asked them.

"Heard what?" Jessica questioned.

"Heard about the big dance at Cedars Hall," they screamed.

"Where is Cedars Hall?" Hortense asked.

"Oh." The girl standing around began to laugh. "You all must be newcomers at Wilshire Academy."

"Everybody knows about the fantastic dances is at Cedars Hall," one girl praised.

"So, tell us more about it," Hortense inquired.

All at once, Professor Higginbotham entered the classroom. He walked in very briskly, tapped his rod on the desk and instructed the students to get seated and get out their calculus books for class instructions.

Jessica Leigh whispered to Hortense, "He talks so fast. I can hardly keep up."

"Don't worry...I'll catch you up when we get back to the room," Hortense promised.

Professor Higginbotham continues to explain a problem on the board with chalk and lecture notes. He is describing how to formulate axioms. When the class was finished, the girls were walking back to the dormitory. As usual, Jessica Leigh was complaining about the calculus class.

"Aunt Martha did not teach me anything. I am completely lost in this class. She worked all summer, but Professor Higginbotham must be well over my head," Jessica murmured.

"Don't worry," Hortense answered her. "You will do fine."

As the girls entered the dormitory, flags and posters

were everywhere.

"Hey," Jessica said as she noticed the flyers.

"Here is some information about the party at Cedars Hall. It's a fall festival for freshman, a get-acquainted dance for students at Wilshire Academy being hosted by the freshman class at West Virginia University. The buses will be parked at the reception hall at 6:30 p.m. The dance is over at twelve midnight, and the buses will bring the students back by 12:30 a.m. You register through your dormitory sisters, and they will present a list to the bus drivers. Well, what do you think?" Jessica Leigh asked.

"Well," Hortense replied. "I'm not going. I don't want to go to any old dance. Besides, I have a physics and chemistry exam next week, and I need to spend all my time studying."

"Hmmm," Jessica followed. "It might be fun."

That night, as the girls were getting ready for bed, Mary Margaret and Elizabeth were huddled together on the top of Mary Margaret's bunk bed. They were whispering to each other and laughing.

"What's so funny?" Jessica asked.

"Oh, nothing," Elizabeth replied.

They kept laughing. "Come on." Jessica pushed them. "We want to be in on the joke."

"Well," Mary Margaret reluctantly answered. "Did you see all the flyers in the front hall talking about the fall harvest dance?"

"Yes," Jessica answered. "The one at Cedars Hall. What is Cedars Hall, anyway?"

Then the girls burst out laughing. "Oh, you would never understand."

Elizabeth laughed.

"Yes," Mary Margaret added. "It's only the most exclusive boys in West Virginia, and only the elite attend. I'm sure you would never fit in with that type. You are not thinking about going, are you?"

"Well, no," Jessica responded. "Not really. I just read the posters."

Then Jessica stared at both girls on the top bunk and asked, "Are y'all going?"

"Of course," the girls replied at the same time.

"My mother has been talking about Cedars Hall for years," Mary Margaret bragged.

"She's bringing two dresses up for me to choose from, and I'll decide which gown to wear."

"Just look in my closet," Elizabeth added with pride. "I've got several formals to choose from."

Then Elizabeth sarcastically asked, "If by some chance you went, Jessica Leigh, what would you wear?"

"Dungarees and suspenders!" Mary Margaret hollered, and the girls jumped off the top bunk and ran down the hall to the bathrooms, laughing all the way.

"They are so mean," Hortense said. "They are so disgustingly mean."

"Well," Jessica Leigh remarked. "I had plenty of practice back home dealing with my cousin, Agnes. She was about as ruthless as these two, but when I put my mind to it, I could pretty well outsmart her. Let me do some thinking."

"About what?" Hortense questioned.

"I may just show up at Cedars Hall after all and show them a thing or two," Jessica responded.

"What are you going to do?" Hortense inquisitively

asked.

"Well, I don't know yet...but I've got a few things in mind." Jessica Leigh smiled at herself. Hortense figured it would be good.

The next day, Hortense and Jessica were walking to class.

Jessica remarked, "You know, Hortense, as I was leaving this morning, I noticed at the sign out desk that there was a list of girls who have signed up for the dance at Cedars Hall."

"Did you see Mary Margaret's or Elizabeth's name?" Hortense asked.

"Yes," Jessica acknowledged. "As a matter of fact, their names were the first two names on the top of the sheet."

"So, what does that mean?" Hortense questioned. "Well..." Jessica Leigh hesitated a second. "I could always erase the names at the top of the sheet and put my name and your name in their place."

Hortense immediately snapped, "Count me out! I told you I didn't want to go to any old dance."

"Well," Jessica Leigh replied. "I think I'm going to do just that. I'm going to sneak in there tonight, erase their names and put my name in. I do not think it will be noticed because there are three sheets of names, and once I erase their names and put my name in, nobody will know what happened."

"You'd better be careful," Hortense warned. "They will be furious."

"Tomorrow is the deadline date to sign up," Jessica reassured her. "And Sister Althea will be removing the list of names. I feel sure they will not even suspect anything. Nobody will know what happened."

"And when the bus arrives at 6:30 p.m. at the reception hall, Mary Margaret and Elizabeth's names will not be on the list," Jessica explained. "So, I guess they can't go! Too bad, so sad."

Hortense again responded, "They will kill you when they find out."

"Don't worry," Jessica Leigh reassured Hortense. "Everything will be okay."

The buses were all lined up at 6:30 p.m. prompt. The reception hall was bustling with activity, and the girls were eagerly waiting. Mary Margaret and Elizabeth were scurrying everywhere. It was obvious that these two were the most glamorous freshman attending the dance. Then Sister Althea appeared, bringing the list of names of students attending the dance.

"Sister, Sister! Look at my gown," Mary Margaret insisted. "Mother had it sent from Paris."

Sister Althea looked puzzled and thought to herself, Oh well, maybe I overlooked her name.

After all thirty-seven girls had signed the list, and she had only reviewed the list once before I send it to the college at Morgantown.

"Oh, yes," she replied. "It is very pretty."

Sister Althea went directly to the bus driver, Sister Adeline. The two ladies were well-acquainted with each other. After all, this Fall Festival had been going on for well over seven years. The Fall Festival is a well-publicized event. The young men and young ladies look forward to this formal dance from the time they were accepted to Wilshire Academy or West Virginia College. The young men and young women were well screened for this event for potential sorority sisters and fraternity brothers. If you wanted to be recognized as somebody, then your appearance at the Fall Festival was imperative.

As a matter of fact, it was probably an unspoken requirement for all freshmen if you had a sorority or fraternity in mind. Only the upper class and the most influential family names made the cut. Your family names and fortunes were certainly used as the criteria on who was chosen for the better sororities or fraternities. Also, your family investment to the academies proved very advantageous in the selection process. So again, The Fall Festival was a major event for all the young men and women who plan to attend.

After Sister Althea and Sister Adeline conversed a while and went over the list of girls attending the dance, Sister Althea called the girls.

"Come this way, girls come this way. As I call your name, you will enter the bus. Each girl I call will be paired with their name after her name. You two girls will ride together on the bus to the dance, and you'll sit in the same seat with the same partner when you return from the dance. Do you understand? You will be accountable, and you must be seated with your partner on the same seat when you return."

"Sister Adeline has the same list I have, and she knows where you will be seated coming and going!"

All the girls were huddled around the bus as Sister Althea began to call out each name. Sister Althea began the call out each name. The first name she called out was Jessica Leigh Staunton and Isabella Brantley.

When Jessica and Isabella walked toward the bus, Mary Margaret whispered to Elizabeth, "Doesn't she look awful?!

That plaid skirt and denim shirt is so countrified."

"Yes," responded Elizabeth. "I wouldn't be caught dead in that outfit, much less be going to a formal affair."

"Hey," Mary Margaret reacted in a puzzle manner. "Weren't our names first on the list?"

"I guess," Elizabeth responded. "She's calling the last girls who signed up first. That way we will be on the front row of the bus."

"I guess you're right, Elizabeth," Mary Margaret agreed. "Besides, we will outshine all the rest of the girls, anyway. They look so tacky."

Then Sister Althea continued to call the next pair of girls. All the other girls were eagerly lined up to take their places on the bus. Fat girls, skinny girls, cotton dresses, taffeta dresses, long dresses, and short dresses. All the girls were excited about the first event at Wilshire Academy.

Sister Althea was almost at the end of the list. She and sister Adeline compared each name as the girls entered the bus.

"Well," Sister Althea remarked. "I guess that's all." Then the two women noticed two girls were still standing: Mary Margaret and Elizabeth Roshavich.

"What about us?" Mary Margaret and Elizabeth cried.

"Well, er...er..." Sister Althea questioned. Then she looked at Sister Adeline and said, "Are they on your list?"

"Let me look over it again," Sister Adeline responded. "I don't think so."

Meanwhile, both girls were grumbling and fussing. "I'd better be on that list! My mother will sue this whole blooming school," Mary Margaret hollered.

"Yes," Elizabeth agreed. "And if I'm not on the list, my

parents will take me out of this

whole school. Besides, we both signed up; as a matter of fact, we signed up on the first day the list was put out."

Then Sister Althea said, "Girls, your names are not on the list. I cannot allow either of you to get on the bus. The headmaster from West Virginia College only approved those thirty seven names. I'm sorry."

Then Mary Margaret proceeded to get on the bus. "I'm going, anyway!" she exclaimed. "I don't care what that old list says. I'm calling my mother, and she'll straighten you all out." She tried to bust right past Sister Adeline.

Then Sister Althea grabbed her. "I'm sorry," she said. "But rules are rules. You girls are not on the list, and you cannot attend. Come on, I'll walk you girls back to the reception hall."

"Yes!" Elizabeth hollered to Sister Althea. "I'm going to call my daddy. He's not going to be happy."

As the bus was leaving, Jessica Leigh rolled her window down and hollered out the window. "Goodbye, Mary Margaret and Elizabeth. I'm sure we will all have a nice time. Wish you could be with us."

The whole bus started laughing, because all the girls at Wilshire Academy knew Mary Margaret and Elizabeth quite well, and they were all glad that these two missed the Fall Festival in Morgantown. The girls were all excited, anticipating what was going to happen at their first major event at Wilshire Academy. Isabella and Jessica were overjoyed that Mary Margaret and Elizabeth missed this trip, but Jessica never mentioned one word about the mix-up and how it all happened.

Isabella remarked, "Have you ever been with a boy? I

mean, by yourself, well, you know what I mean."

"Heavens no," Jessica answered. "I don't even like boys. When you can ride better, rope better, and hunt better, what do you need one of them for?"

"Well, Jessica, why did you want to come to this event?" Isabella asked.

"Well," Jessica replied. "Just to tell the truth, Mary Margaret and Elizabeth rubbed me so much about not fitting in with the high-fuh-lootin' folks, so I decided to show them a thing or two. I'm going to the dance, and I'm gonna get half the boys from Cedars Hall to be calling me."

"But why would you do that?" Isabella questioned.

"To make them jealous – simply to make them jealous," Jessica answered.

"Oh, well," Isabella added. "I wish you luck."

Then Sister Adeline stood in front of the bus and gave her last-minute instructions to the girls. "Girls, you must return to the bus at 11:30 p.m. prompt. When you enter the bus, you must sit in the same seat as you are now. And, girls, remember you are representing Wilshire Academy, so please be on your best behavior. We have always been pleased with the reputation of the girls from Wilshire Academy, so, please, you girls must set the example for next year's class. Have a good time and remember…don't be late! Be back at 11:30 p.m. sharp."

The girls got off the bus and headed toward Cedars Hall. You could hear the music playing, "My Wild Irish Rose." The barbershop quartet was doing a terrific job. "My Old Irish Rose" was loud and clear and the music put everyone in a relaxed mood. As the girls entered Cedars Hall, "Down by the Old Mail Stream" was playing. Cedars Hall was decorated nicely. On one side of the room was a long table. Punch bowls and cups were placed on each end of the table. In between the bowls were cookies and tiny cakes and all kinds of cheese and crackers. Two of the older women were standing by the punch bowl, pouring punch as children requested. When the girls from Wilshire Academy were all inside the room, they were seated on one side. The young men were already seated in another line adjacent to the girls. Then a verydistinguished and sophisticated elderly man stood up at the podium and greeted all the guests.

"Let me introduce myself. I am Dean Devonshire, and these men are our freshman class of 1902-1903. These are the finest young men you'll ever meet. They are most respected, with outstanding leadership abilities and character traits that any young woman would desire. We want you all to mix and mingle and enjoy the music, refreshments, and simply have fun at our fall festival."

As the music began to play, several young men stood up and stepped over towards the ladies. Approaching the girls, the first three couples began to dance. Seven or eight young men got up and headed toward the punch bowl and refreshments. Slowly the girls began to stand up. Some of the girls went to the powder room, and some of the others moseyed over toward the refreshments.

"Hmm," Jessica said to Isabella. "Let me look this situation over."

"What do you mean?" Isabella asked.

"Well," Jessica responded. "I've got to decide which one of these young men interest me the most. It's easy to tell simply by looking at his clothes, style of hair, and how he carries himself."

"Do you mean his posture?" Isabella asked.

"Yes, precisely, his posture," Jessica Leigh added.

There was a tall thin young man with blond hair standing next to the chair railing. His tweed suit was quite becoming, but it was a little tight. It probably belonged to his older brother, who was somewhat thinner than he was.

"But," Isabella added. "He does have good posture."

"Yes," Jessica agreed. "But look at that boy taking the punch cup – look!" she pointed to him. "His dark auburn hair is so shiny. It looks like he brushed it with lard cakes, then split it down the middle. We certainly do not want to get mixed up with him."

All at once, a young man approached Jessica and Isabella. "Let me introduce myself. I'm J. Pierport Morgan II. My family owns a cooperative financial advising company, and we organize for the Carnegie Steel Company."

"Well," Jessica spoke up. "My name is Jessica Leigh Staunton, and my family owns and runs the largest tobacco plantation and Appaloosa horse farm this side of the Mississippi."

Then Isabella Brantley chimed in. "My great uncle just published his first novel about the American Revolution."

"And just who is your uncle, may I ask?" J. Pierport Morgan questioned.

Isabella answered his question with great authority. "Robert W. Chambers, and the title is Cardigan."

"Well," said J. Pierport Morgan, a little perplexed by the girl's response. "It was nice talking to you."

He made a quick exit to the dance floor, looking for another young lady to intrigue with his family's financial wealth. Cussing under his breath, it was obvious he had not impressed either of these girls.

"What was that all about?" Isabella asked Jessica. "I don't know," Jessica responded.

"Now, back to our conversation. Look at that boy with the plaid shirt and sweater vest."

"Yes, he is tall and handsome, I might add," Isabella remarked.

"Now, watch me Isabella," Jessica instructed her. "Let's see if I can get this one under my belt."

Jessica began to stroll over to the young man, as though she was looking for someone else. His head was turned in an opposite direction, and she bumped into the young man.

"Oh, excuse me, excuse me. I am so sorry." Jessica tried to explain.

"No apology needed," the young man explained. The young man moved to the side to let her by. Then as she turned around the strap on her shoe came loose, and she fell right into his arms.

Looking down at her shoe, she apologized again. "That strap has been bothering me all night. I can't even walk without assistance. I wish I had not worn these silly shoes, especially to a dance."

"Here, let me help you to a chair." the nice young man offered.

"Oh, thank you so much, if it isn't too much trouble," she said and smiled a sweet smile.

"No trouble at all." He smiled back, and he escorted her to a nearby chair.

As he helped her to the seat, he made a reference to her

that his grandmother had been a teacher at Wilshire Academy years ago, and that all of his family expected him to find a young lady at Wilshire Academy and make her his wife. Jessica Leigh rolled her eyes, and then she rolled them again and thought to herself, Lordy, I must have come own too strong. I have already hooked this fella and hope I can get away from him.

The young man then asked, "Can I get you some punch?"

"Please," Jessica answered. "And also get two cookies, one for me, and one for my friend, Isabella Brantley."

Then as he hurriedly went to get the punch and cookies, Jessica grabbed Isabella and ordered her, "Quick, let's go to the powder room. Maybe he will disappear, or maybe we can."

When the young man returned with the refreshments, the two girls were gone.

"Well," he muttered. "Wonder where they went."

Peeking out of the powder room, Isabella said, "He's gone. I don't see him."

"Good, maybe he'll attract someone else," Jessica said hopefully. The two girls eased their way out of the restroom door and headed toward the dance floor. Two young men were standing back to back looking around the dance floor.

Jessica eyed the men and told Isabella, "You take the fatter one, and I'll take the one with the mustache."

"What do I do?" Isabella asked.

"Just stand in front of him until he asks you to dance" was her response. "Can't you tell he's just waiting for an opportunity to meet you? So, go on."

Isabella reluctantly sighed. "Will it work?"

"Yes," Jessica promised. "It will work."

"How can you tell it will work?" Isabella fretted again.

"I can tell by his clothes. I can tell by his haircut and by his posture," Jessica reassured her.

And, sure enough, when Isabella stepped on his foot several times while standing in front of him, he finally asked her to dance and yes, they hit it off and were together the rest of the night. Jessica Leigh brushed her long red hair with her hand and sashayed right in front of the man with the mustache. She batted those eyelashes and smiled really big and looked longingly into his big brown eyes.

"And what is your name?" she asked.

"I'm Anthony F. Lucas II from Beaumont, Texas. How can I help you, ma'am?" he proudly asked.

"Well…we are at a dance," Jessica joked with him.

"That's a good idea," the young man laughed. "So, let's dance."

He took her hand, and they began to dance. He could not dance very well, but, after all, neither could Jessica Leigh. So, they made a fine pair. As they danced, Jessica would brush her small breast next to his chest. He was a big man with broad shoulders, wearing a genuine suede jacket. He seemed to love having her body close to his.

As they danced and the music came to an end, he hated to let her go. When the music stopped, he ushered her over to one of the chairs on the side of the room.

"When can I see you again?" Anthony asked.

"Well…" she hesitated. "I don't know. I really don't know much about our dating policies."

"This I do know!" Anthony firmly exclaimed. "We are having a harvest picnic in October. Would you like to go with me?"

"Probably so" was Jessica's answer.

Then Jessica looked at the big circle clock on the wall.

"Isabella will be looking for me. It is almost 11:30 p.m. We are due back at the bus at 11:30."

Anthony squeezed her hand and whispered, "I've had a great evening. I do hope we can get together again. I would love to see you again."

"Me too," Jessica assured him.

Then Anthony said, "May I call you?"

"Yes, I am living at Wellington Hall."

Then the clock began to chime. It was 11:30 p.m.

Dean Devonshire stood up and announced, "We have enjoyed all the ladies from Wilshire Academy for our first fall dance, and we do hope to see you ladies again. The buses are ready, and you are dismissed."

The girls filed themselves back into the bus, and, sure enough, each girl was accounted for, and each girl was seated in her appropriate seat.

"So…" Jessica Leigh looked at Isabella. "You did have a good time, after all, didn't you?"

Isabella just smiled really big and nodded her head. "He is so nice."

"Where is he from?" Jessica asked.

"Somewhere in Kentucky, someplace called Hensley Settlement," Isabella answered.

"Hensley Settlement?" Jessica quizzed.

"Yes. His family established the settlement, and other people followed," replied Isabella.

Then Isabella asked, "And what about your tall, handsome cowboy?"

"Well," Jessica began. "His name is Anthony Lucas, and

his family is in the oil business in Beaumont, Texas, and yes — he wants to see me again. I can't wait to rub all this in on Mary Margaret and Elizabeth."

"But Jessica—" Isabella started, then asked, "Did you like him at all?"

"Yes, a little. Maybe he'll grow on me. He can shoot and ride, probably better than I can. I think his family is more into the business of oil. They have several oil wells in and around the Houston area, and I think that's pretty well what they do all the time — run those oil wells — but when I get through bragging to Mary Margaret and Elizabeth, they will be so envious and jealous of me that they will be biting nails."

"Oh, yes, Isabella. The dance was very much worth the effort that I put into it," Jessica admitted.

"I'm glad you had a good time, and you did seem to like him a little, at least enough to see him again," Isabella added.

"Yes, maybe." Jessica nodded. "And maybe not."

The girls rode on back to Wilshire Academy.

When the bus arrived back at Wilshire Academy, the girls were much quieter than they were on the way to the dance. As the bus approached the building, Sister Althea met them at the end of the walkway.

Sister Adeline stopped the bus, stepped outside of the bus with her list of names and said, "Yes, they all made it back safely, and I do believe they had a good time."

"Great!" Sister Althea exclaimed. "Let's get them off the bus."

As Sister Althea got back on the bus, she gave the last instructions to the girls.

"We are going to file out in order. We will start at the front of the bus. As you step off the bus, you give me your name, then when you get on the ground, you give Sister Adeline your name. And, girls, we are very proud of you all. Another year has gone by, and the fall dance at West Virginia University at Cedars Hall has been another success. The matrons at the dance said you girls behaved beautifully, and they would love to have you girls come back for the harvest picnic. Thank you for behaving so well. We are so proud of our girls at Wilshire Academy. Thank you again."

As the girls got off the bus, Jessica and Isabella were the last ones to get off. They told all the other girls goodbye, and they headed toward their dorm rooms.

As they departed, Isabella reminded Jessica again, "Be sure and tell me about your roommates and just how sick they are when they hear about your experiences at the dance. Mom and dad are coming in tomorrow. Why don't you meet us and we'll all have lunch together?"

"Great," Jessica promised. "See you all tomorrow."

Most of the dorm lights were out. A few lights, scattered here and there, were lit up for the girls as they returned. Jessica Leigh was beginning to think about what to say to her roommates, back in the room.

"I guess, I'll play humble and act as though the dance was not a great event. And yeah, I won't even tell them about Anthony Lucas, and how he wanted all my attention. I guess it would be better to keep peace in the room rather than cause conflict."

As Jessica Leigh entered the room, the lamp near Mary Margaret's bed was on. Both girls were seated on the bed, and Hortense was sound asleep with her earplugs on the bed.

As soon as she arrived in the room, both girls got up, ran to her, and both girls said, "Tell us about the dance."

Then Jessica asked, "Why didn't you girls go?"

"I really don't know," Mary Margaret replied. "We both signed up on the first day, but when Sister Althea read over the names, our names were left off."

"Oh, yeah," Jessica said. "I saw y'all's names on the list when I signed up. Wonder what happened…"

"We don't know," Elizabeth explained. "But my mother is coming up next week to get some answers. I haven't talked to my father, but he will be mad when he hears about this matter. He'll start cussing."

"Anyway," Mary Margaret interrupted. "Tell us about the dance."

"Well," Jessica explained. "There were a lot of cute boys, but I didn't dance a lot. I guess I didn't look good enough."

The two roommates began to snicker under their breath.

Then Jessica added, "The music was good, and the refreshments were great. That's where I stayed most of the time. I talked to the chaperones, and I enjoyed eating the refreshments."

"Tell us again about the young men," Mary Margaret urged her on.

"Some were shy, and many were quite outgoing. I really don't know much about the them because I didn't talk to them. As I was eating, some of them would come by. I thought they would ask me to dance, but they didn't, so I kept on eating."

"I'm tired," Jessica yawned and murmured to herself.

"And full," Elizabeth added.

"Yes, I am full," Jessica responded. "Full as a tick. I do need to go to bed."

Then Jessica put her gown on and climbed into bed and pretended to be asleep. For the next twenty minutes, Elizabeth and Mary Margaret laughed and laughed.

"I knew she wouldn't fit in," Elizabeth joked and remarked.

"So did I," Mary Margaret added. "I don't know why a hillbilly like her would even think about going to a dance at Cedars Hall."

"I can top that," Elizabeth broke in. "I wonder why Jessica ever thought she would fit in at our Academy — Wilshire Academy is for elite girls, anyway."

"Yes," Mary Margaret agreed. "Elite girls only. But I'm tired — let's go to bed. Goodnight, Elizabeth."

"Goodnight," she responded, and she turned out the light.

Jessica arrived at Medical Science class, room 101, Tuesday and Thursday morning from 8 a.m. to 9 a.m. Jessica Leigh was seated on the last seat in the second row. Doctor McKinley could not see her. If he moved to the east side of the room, he could easily see her in view, but most of the time he stood in front of the podium.

I do not like science class, Jessica thought to herself.

Her thoughts kept flitting back and forth to Cripple Creek and all the fun she and George and Sabrina had had skinny-dipping during those long summer months back home. She well remembered those times when she and Sabrina would hide George's clothes and make him beg and beg for them to give them back.

Then she remembered the time that prissy Miss Agnes got caught in the bushes with Lester Buttimer. They were all picnicking near Cripple Creek when a bush started rumbling. Then lo and behold the bush started rattling. Lester and Agnes had been smooching. We knew they were up to something, because Agnes's blouse was buttoned up all wrong, with two buttons left at the tail of a blouse, and Lester's britches were wrong side out. We knew something was up. As I thought about it over and over, I started chuckling out loud — I could not help myself.

"Miss Staunton, Miss Staunton!" Doctor McKinley announced from the podium.

Jessica immediately stood up next to the side of her desk. "Yes, sir, Doctor McKinley."

"Do I have your attention?" he asked her.

"Yes, sir, yes, sir," she addressed him.

"Well, what was so funny?" he sternly asked.

"Well...well," she hesitated.

"Well, well, what?" he responded. "Let us all in on the joke."

Then he insisted that she share the incident. So, Jessica Leigh began to tell the whole story to Doctor McKinley and the classmates.

"Back at home on Staunton Plantation." She looked around the room. "We love to go swimming in Cripple Creek. We enjoyed going skinny-dipping on hot summer afternoons. We especially enjoyed being mean to my cousin, George. Me and Sabrina would hide his clothes. He would have to get out of the water, buck naked, and scout around looking for his clothes."

Doctor McKinley knew it was time to turn the story off.

"That's enough, Miss Staunton, that's enough."

"But—" she interrupted. "You haven't heard the funniest part when my cousin, Agnes, and Lester Buttimer were caught."

"That's enough, that's enough, sit down and please pay attention to my lecture and refrain from laughing in class."

Doctor McKinley continued to talk about the discovery of the hookworm by Doctor Wardley Stiles. Doctor Stiles said that the so-called poor whites in the South were neither lazy or innately stupid, but were suffering from the effects of the parasite. The Rockefeller Foundation was in the process of starting an anti-hookworm campaign throughout the South to help these poor folks.

Jessica wondered to herself, "Wonder if I caught that parasite? I know I'm not lazy or stupid, but sometimes these classes just bore me to death. I just wish I was back home on Staunton Plantation, enjoying the long rides on Patches and Miss Cadelia and Cotton. l wonder how Cotton's whiskey business is doing, and Rooster— Lord, I miss them all. I know my mother loved her family as much as I love mine back at Staunton. Why would she would have never stayed this place, Wilshire Academy?"

It was Saturday morning, back at Staunton Plantation. Mister Teddy came into the kitchen.

"Morning, Miss Cadelia, have we heard from our girl?"

Miss Cadelia responded, "Not this week, Mister Teddy, but we got a good report last week. Seems like Aunt Martha's visit paid off. Her algebra grade was ranked among the top in the class."

Teddy stated, "I know Carlton will be proud of that. He's such a stickler for good grades."

"He sure is," Miss Cadelia responded. "Why, he even added an extra five dollars on her allowance, and, Mr. Teddy, I even slipped two dollars in myself. Yes, we are proud of that young'un."

Then Carlton walked into the kitchen with a somewhat sly grin on his face.

"Morning, Joe."

Growing up as boys, Carlton had nicknamed Teddy "Joe". He didn't always call him this, just when he was pranking around. By now Teddy was at the breakfast table. Carlton sat down, took out his pipe, and looked Ted in the eye. Miss Cadelia handed Carlton his breakfast, then she went on into the back of the house.

"Carlton, Cotton was picking up supplies yesterday and just happened to spot you near Ms. Anglin's boarding-house. Cotton said it looks pretty serious."

"Who was she, Joe? Anybody I know?" Carlton questioned.

Teddy murmured, "Well, I don't know. Do you remember a Mabel Ashwood? She and mom ran around when they were kids."

Carlton asked, "Was she kind of broad with dark red hair?"

"Yeah," Teddy responded. "She always wore her hair balled up on top."

"I remember. We always hated to sit behind her at mass because you could never see the priest. She must've piled her hair a mile high."

Carlton quickly said, "She did! Mama helped her wash it about twice a year, and her hair came down way below her butt. Yeah, I remember Mabel Ashwood very well. And I do recall she had a girl right cute named Sally Mae or Sally Ann or something another."

Teddy continued to talk. "Well, we were the same age. I kind of liked her. We never went out, except when she sat on grandma's front porch."

"Smooched a little, I'm sure," Carlton added.

"Well, yeah," Teddy agreed. "When grandma wasn't looking. But most of the time she was swinging right along with us on the big front porch."

Carlton then asked, "Where did she run off to?"

"Somewhere in Chicago," Teddy answered.

"What is she doing back home?" he asked.

Teddy then explained, "Her brother sold some of the property, and they needed her back home to fill out some of the legal documents. He sold almost 1,000 acres."

"What did they do with the rest?" Carlton inquired.

Teddy responded, "He's leasing it out. Tobacco prices are a pretty high risk."

Sally said, "They are pretty proud of their investments."

Looking Teddy in the eye, he quizzed him, "Well, Joe, what are your intentions?"

"Don't know just yet," Teddy quickly responded. "You know I have not had a mind for lady folks for quite some time now."

"How does she look?" Carlton asked.

"Rather good to be forty-ish or fifty-ish" was his answer.

"Is the attraction still there?" Carlton pushed for an answer.

"Well, maybe, you know twenty-two years is an awfully long time. Don't know if the eternal flame is still glowing – only time will tell," Teddy admitted.

Miss Cadelia returned to the kitchen with a medical case, overcoat, and a top hat. She then scooped up several biscuits and a slice of cheese. She nicely wrapped a couple of tomatoes and two pieces of fruitcake into a large picnic basket.

"Mister Teddy, I'm not trying to rush you off, but this surgery is scheduled for mid-afternoon. You best be on your way."

"Carlton, I almost forgot."

"Yes," Teddy acknowledged. "Mrs. Cranford's due date is upon us."

"Didn't she have severe complications with the first child?", questioned Carlton. Teddy noted, "Almost died before we did the c-section. We don't want any reoccurrences like that. We are taking the baby a week ahead of time. Just don't want to take any chances."

Teddy looked at Miss Cadelia. "Miss Cadelia, I don't know when I'll be back."

"George will be fine," Miss Cadelia promised. "Sabrina's got to finish her bug collection. It's due next week. She's always depended on me to do her work," Doctor Staunton explained.

"No need to worry, Mister Teddy," Miss Cadelia said. "Me and Sabrina will get the fly net and will have all them bugs collected, stuck, and labeled before you return. I can guarantee you that."

Carlton then questioned, "What about Agnes?"

"She'll be staying with Molly Yergermyer," Teddy told Carlton. "I promised her she could go to that school frolic. There will be plenty of chaperones. I made sure of that before I agreed to let her go. Mr. Yergermyer will pick her up sometimes this morning."

Teddy got up from the table. He went to his bedroom to get a few more personal items, came back down the stairs, then was on his way. He rode off from Staunton Plantation toward Calhoun City. Calhoun City was the next town past Templeton, Virginia. Templeton had no hospital. Calhoun City did have a hospital. George, Miss Cadelia, and Sabrina were out looking for bugs. Sabrina had a large fishnet.

George had an old tin can with the top on it, and Miss Cadelia was carrying a cardboard tray. Each time they caught an insect, Cadelia suffocated it with liniment and alcohol, then she stuck the bug on the cardboard tray with a straight pin. Sabrina was scampering throughout the meadow near Staunton Plantation chasing butterflies. George had an old stick, and he was prying around near an old oak tree looking for stinkbugs. When he found one, he picked it up and stuck it into the tin can. Miss Cadelia was sitting on the tree stump. When the children got an insect, they brought it to her. She dipped the bug into the solution, then pierced the pin through the bug and pinned the bug to the cardboard. George got excited. He grabbed up two lizards and was carrying them to Miss Cadelia. Miss Cadelia kindly explained that a lizard is not an insect. Looking down at the cardboard, Miss Cadelia had Sabrina label each insect.

1. Beetle
2. Honeybee
3. Browntail moth
4. Mosquito
5. Horsefly
6. Ant

7. Dragonfly
8. Grasshopper
9. Yellow jacket
10. Katydid
11. Cockroach
12. Army worm

They were working on the bug collection, when Rooster runs toward them hollering.

Miss Cadelia questioned, "Rooster, what are you hollering about? Can't you see we are doing our book work? We got to tag these bugs before Mr. Teddy returns!"

Rooster began hollering again, "That gal! It's that gal – woman – that Mr. Teddy knows from Chicago."

Cadelia stood up and looked down the road in order to see the fancy carriage heading toward them. The kids all ran toward Miss Cadelia. Everybody wanted to see who the lady visitor was. She wasn't dressed like a tobacco farmer; in fact, she didn't even look like anybody from around these here parts. The fancy wagon had two thoroughbred quarter horses pulling the it.

There was a part over the wagon, either to keep the sunshine from getting in her eyes, or to prevent rain from getting her hair wet, anyhow, the wagon stopped and the lady introduced herself.

"I am Sally Mae Ashwood, a long-time acquaintance of Doctor Theodore Staunton. I was informed that he might just possibly be out here visiting his brother."

Then Cadelia spoke up. "Ma'am, I can't tell you when he might return. The doctor had to go to Calhoun City. However, seeing that you have come out this far, would you like to come in and rest a while? Then you can start back toward town."

Miss Ashwood hesitated and then said, "Why, yes. That might be nice."

Then Miss Cadelia explained, "I am Cadelia, Mr. Staunton's housekeeper. Please come on up to the house and join us, perhaps even stay for dinner."

The children stared at the nice wagon. Then Miss Ashwood could see the children were fascinated with the fancy wagon.

She asked, "Would the children like to ride back with me?"

Miss Cadelia quickly responded, "No, ma'am, they can walk back."

Then she told the children, "Scoot on back toward the house."

But Sabrina jumped up so fast into the wagon that Miss Cadelia could not stop her.

Sabrina answered, "Yes, ma'am —I'd love to ride back with you."

Then Sabrina smiled really big. Sabrina loved the wagon, and she seemed to have a special liking for Miss Sally Mae Ashwood. When the fancy carriage pulled up to the front of Staunton Plantation, Carlton heard all the commotion. The field hands saw the fancy carriage pulling up, and naturally they were all impressed, and wanted to see what special person was arriving.

Carlton went out to the carriage and introduced himself, "And you must be Sally Ann Ashwood. Your mother was Mabel Ashwood."

"Yeah, but I am Sally Mae. I have a cousin named Sally

Ann, but she was from Calhoun City. I came to see Doctor Staunton. I'm staying at Miss Anglin's boarding house, and I ran into your brother. He invited me out here."

"Good, Miss Ashwood. Do come in, Teddy is not here right now."

"Yes," Miss Cadelia mentioned. "He has gone to Calhoun City to deliver a baby."

Then Miss Cadelia spoke up to Miss Ashwood. "Why don't you come in and rest a while. Here, let me help you out of that carriage. We will enjoy your coming in and visiting awhile."

Quickly, Sabrina said, "I like you, Miss Ashwood."

"Thank you," Miss Ashwood responded, and Carlton helped Sally Mae out of the carriage and into the house.

Meanwhile, Rooster and George finally arrived back home. Miss Cadelia came in the side door and asked Carlton if they would like anything to eat.

"I'll ask her," Carlton answered. "Right now she is freshening up from the ride out here. I'll ask her when she comes out."

Sally Mae and Carlton are seated in the parlor drinking cool water and eating a slice of homemade peach cobbler.

Carlton spoke up. "Teddy says you are leasing some of your land to the tobacco planters."

"Yes, John David sold quite a bit of land, but we are going to lease well over 500 acres, and he needed my signature on the papers."

"Who will be leasing the property?" Carlton inquired.

"Don't know yet – several prospects have inquired, but John David has not made up his mind," she replied.

"Well," Carlton stated. "This is a good time to lease. Prices are high, at the top market price."

Changing the subject, Carlton said, "I was simply interested, how long are you going to be here?"

Sally Mae looked at Carlton, stared into his face, and replied, "I really do not know at this time. I've been working for the WW industries…Workers of The World. My contract ran out several months ago, and I don't know if I want to be involved for another year. Yes, it is such a demanding job. The rules have tightened, and President Roosevelt is requiring the Wooblies to sign forms of retaliation if any disturbances break out. So, I really don't know what my situation is thus far."

"Well, if you decide to stay here, I'm sure you'll be able to find a job, with your experience you could probably do almost anything," Carlton explained.

"Well," Sally Mae reacted. "I just may be looking." Then she asked, "Do you think Doctor Staunton could use a receptionist? I am good at making appointments."

Carlton laughed and said, "I'm sure Teddy would love to have you around. Hope it works out."

Then Sally Mae stood up. "I guess I'll be getting on back to Templeton."

Carlton escorted her to the carriage.

Miss Cadelia came out to the carriage and said, "Miss Ashwood, do come back. We would love to have you come out for dinner."

"Why, thank you, Miss Cadelia," Miss Ashwood responded. "I would love to do just that. Goodbye, Carlton, tell Teddy I'm sorry I missed him."

"Oh," Carlton vowed. "He'll be sorrier than you are that

he missed you. Do come again and enjoy a meal with us."

Carlton helped Miss Ashwood into the carriage, and she rode back to Templeton.

Back at Wilshire Academy, the girls were on an outing to the harvest picnic at West Virginia University hosted by the boy's freshman class. As the girls got off the bus from Wilshire Academy, the young men began to approach the designated area. Jessica Leigh was a little hesitant.

She said, "I hope I can remember what he looks like."

"I'm sure you can," Isabella assured her. "I thought about nothing but Charles Hensley. I can see every feature on his face...his curly light brown hair, his plump little face, and his pearly white teeth. I do wish he were a little taller. I hate to tower over him, if I had elevated pumps on."

As the two girls walked toward the pavilion, they noticed how beautiful the campus looked. West Virginia University was founded in 1867 in Morgantown, West Virginia. Anthony had told Jessica Leigh that the harvest picnic is always hosted on the east side of the campus. Trees were scattered all over the grounds.

"I love the trees." Isabella said. She knew the American Basswood because the scent of the honey flowers from the tree permeated the entire area.

"Oh, there's Charles Hensley now." And, sure enough, his pearly white teeth and dimples shined in the November sun, as he approached Isabella and Jessica Leigh.

"There you are!" he screamed, and he hurriedly ran toward Isabella and grabbed her hand as he picked her up off the ground. He was very excited to see her.

Then Isabella asked, "Do you remember Jessica Leigh?"

"Oh, yes," he replied. "So nice to see you again. I know

Tony is very excited that you decided to come."

"Where is he, anyway?" Jessica asked.

"Oh," Charles replied. "He's in the rugby competition."

As they looked to the other side, you could see a group of boys playing with a bat and an oblong ball.

"He told me to tell you to stay with us until the game is over."

"Let's go over there," Jessica interrupted. "I'd like to watch them play."

"Good." Charles smiled, and the three of them walked toward the rugby football game.

"What is the game called?" Jessica inquired.

"Football," Charles answered. "Rugby football originated from the United Kingdom."

Then Charles began to explain how one team competes against another team to push the

football across the opposing team's line. As they approached the competition, Anthony looked up and saw them coming towards the field.

He hollered, "Jessica! Jessica!"

She waved both hands, and he went back to playing with the group.

"Looks dangerous, if you ask me," Isabella said.

"Oh," Charles quickly responded. "These fellows are tough. They can handle it."

As Jessica Leigh looked around the grounds, she noticed beautiful quilts scattered all over the grounds.

"Who do the quilts belong to?" she asked.

"Oh," Charles explained. "That's the auxiliary, the Harvest Festival Auxiliary. The ladies spend all year working on these beautiful quilts just for this special occasion."

"Well, they are fine, such exquisite detail," she added.

"The game is about over," Charles said. Then he explained, "Dean Devonshire made a direct point to instruct the rugby coaches that when the girls arrived from Wilshire the rugby game must be over."

"I guess," Charles admitted. "The game must be running a little slow."

"Oh, that's all right," Jessica responded. "I'm enjoying observing the beautiful campus, and looking at the paddle boats over there."

A small stream ran right through the side of the campus, and the stream had lots of brightly colored paddle boats floating in the water.

Charles interjected, "We also enjoy riding in the paddle boats after the picnic. It's been a tradition ever since the school was built."

By now the campus was filled with young men and women, teachers and professors, all leisurely meandering through out the beautiful grounds. Red Maple and American Sycamore trees made a great shade for the quilts on the ground. The couples began to unfold their picnic baskets and enjoy their delicious lunches.

Finally, the games ended, and Anthony Lucas ran to join Jessica Leigh, Isabella, and Charles. He was so pleased to see her. Jessica Leigh knew all along that she would be coming to the picnic, but she did not give him her final answer until last week. He was grinning from ear to ear. He went straight to Jessica Leigh, put his arms around her, and hugged her tight. She had to maneuver herself to get out of his control.

"I love the beautiful campus," she remarked.

"Yes, it is so nice. It's a joy in class time to watch out the windows and to watch the seasons change. Weather here is so different from Texas weather," Anthony exclaimed.

As they were walking hand-in-hand, Jessica Leigh spotted Mary Margaret and Elizabeth. She knew they had signed up for the picnic, first on the list of course. This time Jessica Leigh did not even mention to them that she was going to picnic. When Mary Margaret saw Jessica Leigh with a good-looking, handsome rugby football player, she was rather shocked. Mary Margaret and Elizabeth were with two boys, seated on a quilt with the picnic basket.

"Oh, my goodness," Isabella whispered. "There's that young man who was looking for a wife, do you remember him?"

"I sure do," Jessica Leigh responded quickly. "Let's stay clear from them."

"What are y'all talking about?" Anthony asked.

"Nothing, nothing…just nothing," Jessica Leigh responded. All at once Jessica Leigh heard her name being called.

"Oh, Jessica! Oh, Jessica!" Mary Margaret hollered to Jessica Leigh.

Mary Margaret stood up and raced straight toward Jessica Leigh.

"Well, if it isn't my little old roommate, Jessica Leigh Staunton. I didn't know you were coming today! I would have saved you a spot at our special quilt."

Then Mary Margaret sashayed up to Anthony, batted her big blue eyes at him and asked, "Who might you be?"

"Oh, I'm Anthony Lucas," he answered.

Mary Margaret did not waste one minute. She grabbed Anthony's arm and demanded, "You all come sit with us."

Then she dragged Anthony over to her quilt. Reluctantly, Anthony followed her.

"My mama sent a great picnic lunch — strawberry muffins, ladyfingers, cheddar pop-overs, and featherlight puffs made right from her own oven."

"You all sit down," Elizabeth coaxed the others.

Isabella and Jessica Leigh looked disgusted and outdone.

Then Elizabeth spied Charles, she quickly said, "You can sit right here, and what is your name?"

He reluctantly answered, "Charles," then he said, "But… but…"

"But nothing," Elizabeth answered back to him. "We can all enjoy this picnic lunch together."

Then Mary Margaret turned to the boy who was seated next to her. "Albert," she said. "Go get something cool for us to drink."

Then Elizabeth added, "And why don't you take Lester Lee with you?"

Isabella and Jessica Leigh knew immediately that the conniving roommates had planned to dump their fellow friends and steal the young men who had come with Jessica Leigh and Isabella. Mary Margaret looked perfect in her orange and lilac corduroy-gathered skirt with the trim lace around the white cotton blouse that she was wearing. And Elizabeth Roshavick looked like all rich, Jewish girls. Her imported shoes and custom-made garment were from Hong Kong. There was no way you could outlook either of these two girls.

"Anthony," Mary Margaret began to brag to him. "I love the beautiful gardens here on campus. They are always so colorful, no matter what season you view them."

"When did you see them?" he questioned. "Why, I've been on this campus many times, Mother and father are personal friends of the president. My father is on the Board of Directors."

"Oh, really?" Anthony replied. Then he said, "Here, Jessica Leigh, you can come sit next to me." He scooted over to save her a space next to him, Then Elizabeth noticed that Isabella was still standing next to the quilt.

Appearing not to be rude, Elizabeth spoke up. "You can sit down. We're not excluding you."

Isabella just looked disgusted. Yeah, she thought to herself. You would if you could.

By then, Albert and Lester Lee were bringing all the drinks back to the group, "Lemonade! Lemonade! Cool, cool, lemonade," Lester Lee announced.

"Thanks." Mary Margaret grabbed two of the drinks. She handed one to Anthony, and she kept one for herself.

Anthony knew he and Charles had made a big mistake by ending up at this particular quilt, with Mary Margaret and Elizabeth.

Then Lester Lee said, "Move over, Charles. She's with me."

Then he squeezed himself right next to Elizabeth and wrapped his arm around her shoulders.

"Anything else you need, sugar?" Lester Lee asked.

Jessica Leigh and Isabella chuckled to each other.

That will take care of Elizabeth. That fella, Lester Lee won't let her out of his sight, they thought to themselves.

Isabella said, "Lester Lee is after a wife."

Jessica Leigh and Isabella were just proud that Lester Lee had not chosen either of them for his wife. All at once the music began to play, and a small horse-drawn wagon was making its way through the crowds. The small four-man band was singing and playing their instruments. One young man was on the harmonica — one was playing the fiddle, and one was strumming the banjo. The last man was the lead singer. As they made their way through the crowds, people began to sing and chant with them. I do believe the small four-man band was a success, because throughout the entire evening you could hear the music as the wagons strolled throughout the West Virginia campus. Anthony and Jessica Leigh began to eat some of the things that Jessica Leigh had brought in her picnic basket – homemade tea cookies, pomegranate jam, and biscuits.

There were several gazebos set up all over campus, where you could get chicken wings and chicken legs, roast beef slices, and ham. Fresh fruit was also offered along with bread of every type, plenty of varieties of pudding, pies, even homemade candies were offered at the gazebo stands. The Ladies Auxiliary always provided meals for the students who live too far away to provide their own lunches. Many of the boys lived hundreds of miles from campus, and their families could not assist them at these picnic affairs. So, the Ladies Auxiliary always provided the delicious meals for the picnic menu. Elizabeth was beginning to get agitated. Lester Lee would take a bite of bread, then he would take the same piece of bread and try to feed it to Elizabeth Ann.

"Were just made for each other," Lester Lee remarked.

"My grandmother knew I would meet the lady of my dreams, and Elizabeth Ann, you are the lady."

He bent over and kissed her. Elizabeth Ann just smiled, and sneakily took Charles's hand and winked at him. Isabella stood up. "Now I've had enough. I saw that."

She made her point directly to Elizabeth. "Oh," Elizabeth Ann admitted. "I was just kidding."

She turned to Lester Lee and put both arms around him and smacked him on the lips. It must've been a good kiss because they were embracing for well over thirty seconds.

Then Elizabeth Ann got up, straightened her dress, and demanded, "Come on, Lester Lee. Let's take a walk."

Lester Lee then remarked, "Isabella must have personal problems, I'm sure. I do not know what's gotten into her."

Then Lester Lee took Elizabeth's hand, and the two of them strolled toward the paddle boats. Elizabeth Ann glared back at Charles and motioned with her mouth.

"I'll see you later." Isabella saw what she had mouthed to him.

"Don't worry, Isabella." Charles spoke up quickly. "I have no interest in her. Besides, Lester Lee will not let her out of his sight."

"How does she know you, Charles?" Isabella asked.

Then he answered, "Our families are old friends. Some type of family connection, family ties – we've known each other for years."

Then Charles continued, "Lester Lee's grandparents visited the Hensley community in Kentucky, a widowed aunt of Lester Lee had married one of the nephews, Best friends, I think – that's the story, and it goes back a long way. I think Lester Lee thinks he's caught an angel straight from heaven."

Then Isabella added, "Yeah, but did he see her horns and red tail and the pitchfork she carries?"

They both laughed, and Isabella was glad that Elizabeth Ann was gone for now, that is.

The rest of the meal was relatively pleasant. Mary Margaret did her best to put on her best behavior.

Talking in her softest voice and smiling, she gazed at Anthony Lucas. "I just love the rugby sport now, Anthony."

Mary Margaret praised him. "You must be awfully strong and smart to play such a dangerous sport." Then she used both of her hands to feel his strong arm muscles.

"Well," Alfred interrupted quickly. "I play soccer. I play soccer, and I am so strong!"

Mary Margaret turned to Alfred and murmured, "That's nice." Then she turned back to Anthony to focus her attention back on him.

She asked, "Anthony Lucas, what does your family do?"

"We are in the oil business from Beaumont Texas," he replied.

Again, Mary Margaret beamed with joy and said, "My, my, I'll never understand how my little old roommate Jessica Leigh attracted such a distinguished young man like yourself."

Then she turned to Alfred. "Come on, Alfred, let's walk through the garden. My mother was responsible for the layout of the gardens. She and her club members designated which plants would be placed where. My mother is so intelligent. She can do anything, and I am sure I'll follow in her footsteps."

As Mary Margaret stood up, Albert was quick to assist

her. She looked at Anthony and smiled. "Tootle-loo! We will see you later."

"Nice meeting you," Anthony said.

"Good riddance," Jessica murmured to herself under her breath.

"What did you say? What did you say?" Mary Margaret questioned.

"Nothing – nothing." Jessica answered. Then Jessica read Anthony's mind. "She made you sick, didn't she, Anthony?" Jessica remarked.

"Yes, she did," he acknowledged that fact. "But I figured I would be polite since she is your roommate."

"You are so right," Jessica admitted. "I do have to room with her, so I do try to get along. Let's just forget about her; let's just relax on the quilt. I need a soft pillow."

He looked at Jessica. Jessica knew exactly what he meant, and she scooted over toward him, and he put his head on her lap, and he looked gazingly into her eyes.

"I've waited all month to see you again. I was afraid you might not come today," he exclaimed.

"Well," Jessica responded. "I had been feeling a bit under the weather, and I didn't want to obligate myself and then disappoint you."

Then Anthony put his arms up and drew her face next to his, and they kissed.

Jessica didn't realize exactly how strong he was, and she really enjoyed the warmth of his lips on hers, but she didn't want to let him know how much she really enjoyed the kiss, so she slowly jerked away, then she noticed and said, "Isabella and Charles have gone. They must have wandered away. Wonder where they went?"

"Probably," Anthony replied. "Toward the paddle boats. That's the normal procedure here at the University. The couples paddle down the winding stream that encircles most of the campus."

Then he drew her back into his embrace and kissed her again.

The winding stream was full of paddle boats, floating along. Each sailboat was decorated with beautiful flags, flowing as the boats made their way along the stream. Each boat had either two or four passengers. The young men sat on one end, rowing the boats, while the young ladies sat on the other end facing their dates. The day had turned out to be a lovely day for a picnic and a boat ride. Jessica Leigh and Anthony were strolling along. She was holding his hand, and on and off she would lay her head on his shoulders.

Yes, Jessica Leigh began to think to herself, maybe I am in love – I just may be in the love – oh, well.

When they reached the stream, several boats were lined up on the shoulders.

"Would you like to go for a ride?" Anthony asked her.

"Of course I would. I understand this is a major event here at the University," Jessica Leigh said approvingly.

"Yes, that's what they all tell me. As a matter of fact, the saying goes that you take a Wilshire Academy young lady on the paddle boat, and you are guaranteed that she'll eventually become your bride, so, Jessica Leigh, are you sure you want to make that commitment?" Anthony earnestly asked.

"Oh, Tony," Jessica Leigh blurted. "We do not even know each other."

Then he answered, "I know enough, and Jessie?"

He then looked into her eyes and admitted, "I do love you," and he drew her into his arms and they kissed again. This time she did not try to squirm out of his hold. She just relaxed and enjoyed the romantic kiss.

Just then, Charles and Isabella's boat drifted toward them.

"Hurry up, you lovebirds!" Charles hollered.

At that, Anthony and Jessica parted from their embrace and got into the empty boat. Anthony helped her into the boat and got her seated. He got in the other side, and the two of them rode out toward Charles and Isabella.

"Let's race," Charles called to Anthony.

"Okay!" he responded. "Let's line up and be sure we have a clear path. We certainly do not want any accidents!" Anthony hollered back. Charles agreed.

The two rowboats lined up side-by-side.

Jessica Leigh said, "I'll say on your mark— get set — go!"

Both of the paddle boat started off. Anthony was a bit stronger than Charles, so the yellow paddleboat got off to a quick start.

"Hurry, hurry!" Jessica hollered. "We must beat them."

"Hey, where do you want to race to?" Charles asked.

Hollering back, Anthony exclaimed, "Down by the old hollow log, right after Devil's Bend."

"Okay," Charles answered.

Anthony sped up, and he and Jessica Leigh were off, five or six yards ahead. Jessica Leigh waved toward the other paddle boats. She was beaming with pride as she and Anthony rode much more swiftly and sped past the other competitors on the stream. Jessica was smiling as her long, red hair flowed, tossing and turning in the wind. The race was on, and Anthony's strong arms and muscles showed those of a true athlete. Jessica noticed that the muscle tone in his legs was very structured. Yes, it was obvious that Anthony was in excellent physical condition. Several other paddle boats were making their journey down the stream.

The boats were two seaters or four seaters, and a colored flag was attached to each boat: yellow, red, orange, blue, and green. The weather was very pleasant, and the paddle boat rides are a great ending for the Harvest Picnic. By the time Jessica and Anthony reached the old hollow log, beyond Devil's Bend, the sun was beginning to make its way behind the clouds.

Anthony stopped the boat, stood up and said, "Jess, there is the hollow log, Charles told us to stop when we got here. An old tree must have fallen many years ago into the stream, and over the years the water flow had cut deep into the trunk. Now, all that is left is the old hollow log, protruding out from the embankment."

"Let's get out, Anthony, and sit and wait for Isabella and Charles," Jessica requested.

Anthony just smiled and eased the paddleboat toward the embankment. There were a lot of bushes and brush tangled in and around the trunk. A tiny white bloom covered most of the brush.

As Jessica looked around, she commented, "It's so pretty and peaceful at this particular location. How did this location ever get associated with the name, Devil's Bend?"

Then Anthony looked at Jessica and said, "This spot is very romantic, wouldn't you say?"

"Why, yes, but as I ask you how does Devil's Bend fit into the picture?" Jessica persistently asked again.

Then after Anthony tied the paddleboat to a sturdy limb growing from the embankment, he eased over from his seat to the other side of the paddleboat to her seat. Jessica immediately scooted over to give him room to sit next to her.

"Well, you see, years ago the Shawnee Indians lived in these parts. White Union soldiers convinced these people that they needed to leave the territories, because the White Devil was going to destroy their people unless they left the area."

"And who was the White Devil?" Jessica asked.

"Oh, Jessica, you know there was no White Devil, but the story frightened the Indians anyway."

Jessica moved closer to Anthony. Immediately, he started to embrace her small body. His kisses were so strong and warm as he encircled her mouth. One of his hands slowly caressed her right breast. Jessica curved herself more into his body, and she didn't resist his exploring hand. All at once, several paddle boats were paddling upstream, and the boats spotted Jessica and Anthony, seated on the embankment. The boys in the paddleboats began to holler. The boys all had on Indian headbands and feathers.

"Enough of that you two, enough of that!"

While his right hand began to feel for her breasts, he was very gentle as he caressed her other breast, and he rubbed her breast from side to side. Then he took both hands and squeezed Jessica's waist really tight.

She was really enjoying the moment. Jessica continued to kiss him by placing her tongue in his mouth. She was moving with excitement as both bodies embraced with sexual arousal. All at once, they were interrupted again by the screaming and chanting Indians.

"None of that, none of that."

When Anthony looked around, several of his rugby team players were headed toward them paddling upstream. Jessica drew herself away from Anthony in embarrassment.

"Don't worry about them," Anthony assured her. "Don't worry about them."

All the paddle boats were headed toward them, and Anthony said reluctantly, "Guess I have to introduce you. They have been ribbing me since the fall dance."

The four rugby boys were in a paddleboat heading toward Jessica and Anthony.

"Come on, Tony," one boy said. "You can't get by that easy. We caught y'all. We've got you all circled."

The four boys tied their boat to the boat ramp near the old hollow log. Then they jumped out of their paddle boats and headed toward the old tree trunk, where Jessica was still seated and Anthony had stood up. Two tall, lanky dark-skinned boys approached Jessica Leigh. One of the young men was standing with one foot on the log and the other foot on the front of Anthony's boat. The boy was bent over trying to get a good look at Jessica.

"Let me get a good look at you, gal," he snapped. Jessica knew he had been drinking because the alcoholic aroma consumed the area as he talked to her.

Then the other boy jumped into the boat and said, "I swear, Tony, I swear I see why you've been so quiet-mouthed about this girl. If she were my girl, I'd keep it a secret, too."

Tony then helped Jessica stand and said, "I'd like you to meet my fraternity brothers, Alan and Mitch. Alan and I are from the same hometown – Beaumont, Texas – and Mitch's family is from Austin, Texas."

"Oh!" Jessica Leigh enthusiastically exclaimed. "So nice to meet you fellows."

One boy teased Anthony, "We saw you at the Harvest Carnival dance at Cedars Hall, but Tony gave us strict instructions to stay away."

Finally, the other two boys joined the group. They had been splashing each other with their paddles from the boat. They were pushing each other, rousting and tussling.

Then Anthony introduced them. "This is Troy Bartholomew. Troy is from Jersey, and Alex is a Boston aristocrat, or he thinks he is."

Then Anthony joked, "You guys don't have a date. No wonder! No woman could stand

being around you guys for an hour much less a whole day."

"You're right! You're right!" Alex admitted. "That's why we tracked you all down. We figured Jessica would share part of y'all's time with us."

"All kidding aside," Alex said. "We are very pleased to meet you. Tony is very fond of you, and we are finally glad to have the opportunity to meet you, and see you and talk with you."

Jessica kind of timidly held her head down and admitted, "I have enjoyed my first semester at Wilshire Academy, and getting to know Anthony has definitely added some fun and excitement in my first experience away from home."

"And where is your home?" Alex asked.

"Staunton, Virginia," she responded.

"Well," Troy spoke up. "You and your family live right around the corner."

"You might say that. It's only 200 miles away," Jessica added.

"Come on, fellows," Alan exclaimed. "Let us leave them alone."

So spontaneously and abruptly they disappeared as quickly as they had appeared. The four boys got back into their paddle boats, and headed on back to the main dock.

Jessica Leigh hollered back to the boys as they left, "Nice to have met you all!"

Anthony echoed back to them, "And nice for you all to leave."

The boys got back to laughing and playing in the boat. It was quite obvious that they were intoxicated, Jessica thought to herself. I agree with Tony – who would want to be stuck with one of them all afternoon? They were all nice-looking gentlemen, but rather obnoxious.

Jessica was just proud that she was with Anthony Lucas. As the boys were heading upstream, another boat was heading down the stream, coming their way. It was Charles and Isabella. Charles did not even look like he had worked up a sweat. He was just meandering down the stream talking ninety to nothing about nothing.

"Well," Anthony hollered to them. "It's about time y'all got here."

Charles answered back, "We've had a good time just talking."

Then Charles and Isabella parked their boat next to

Anthony's. The two of them got out of their boat and sat on the hollow log, next to Anthony's boat. The two couples were planning on spending the rest of the afternoon with each other, enjoying themselves on the water's bank. Charles had his arm around Isabella, whispering in her ear, and Anthony was holding Jessica's hand with both of his hands. Love was in the air.

"Are you looking forward to going home, Jessica?" Anthony asked. "Yes, as a matter of fact, I am looking forward to seeing my family. But I have two exams on Friday before I leave. I do hope I can concentrate and make decent grades."

"Oh," Isabella interrupted. "You'll do fine. You've got an excellent record in both classes, and I'm sure your grades will be at the top of the class."

"I do not know." Jessica hesitated. Then she turned to Anthony and asked, "What are your plans for the holidays?"

"Well," Anthony explained. "Since we only have two weeks for the break, my parents are coming here, and we are going to Jersey for the holidays. Mom has a sister who lives in Newark."

Then Charles interrupted, "Don't forget to tell her about Mitch's mom, she is going to!"

"Oh yeah," Anthony added. "Mitch's mom is coming with them. She has relatives in New Jersey, so mom invited her and Mitch to come with us."

Then Charles had a turn to share his plans for the holidays.

"I dread the holidays! I have a large family. Most of them live in and around Hensley, Kentucky. Twice a year we have a big family reunion. Aunts and cousins, nieces and nephews, lots of family members attend the event. There are a hundred or so, and we all spend two whole days together. Yes, I dread it a lot!"

"Well, it sounds nice to me," Isabella said.

"Well, it isn't. They all asked the same questions and say the same things. 'You look so much like Grandpa Hensley. You have his smile and his pleasant disposition.' And practically all of them say, 'Your grandpa would be so proud of you.' This question always comes up, and 'where do you go to school?' I repeat the same answer over and over and over again, but they keep asking. Some of the older ones forget that they have already asked me the same question."

Then Jessica asked Charles, "What are their intentions for you?"

"Well, of course," Anthony interrupted. "He has to assure them that when he graduates from college, he'll move back to Hensley and carry on the Hensley tradition."

"Yeah, and I get so tired of hearing the same old discussion every time I go home."

Charles just shook his head and said, "They must act like that simply because they are old."

"Yes." Isabella tried to console him. "One day you'll be old, and you'll simply relish in the conversation with young people."

"I guess you are right, Isabella," he said. "Enough talking." He drew her to him and he started kissing her.

Jessica Leigh then stood up, looked at Anthony, and sighed.

"I guess we'd best be getting back to the rest of the group. I haven't noticed any more paddle boats, since Charles and Isabella arrived. They'll probably be wondering where we are. Then Anthony said, "Charles, we are getting ready to go back."

Isabella backed out of the embrace with Charles and said, "Okay, we will go also."

Then both couples got up off the old hollow log and got into their paddle boats, heading back upstream to the boat ramps in the picnic area. As they began to approach shore, who should be waiting on them, hollering and waving their arms all about, but Mary Margaret and Elizabeth Roshavick.

"What could they want?" Jessica Leigh wondered to herself.

Then Isabella saw them, and she said, "Look, there's Mary Margaret and Elizabeth, what could they want?"

As the boats began to get closer to the shore, Jessica began to worry a bit. In the distance she saw Dean Devonshire, Doctor McKinley, and Sister Adeline. She thought to herself, what is Sister Adeline doing here. The picnic was not over until 8 PM, and here was Sister Adeline two hours early.

"Hurry, hurry!" Elizabeth and Mary Margaret hollered. "Hurry!"

"What is this all about?" Anthony questioned.

"I don't know, but it doesn't look good," Jessica responded.

"Did we do something wrong?" Charles wondered to himself.

By the time the two boats got to the boat ramps, both Doctor McKinley and Dean Devonshire were standing on the shore next to the water. As Jessica Leigh got out of the boat, Dean Devonshire approached her, took her to the side and whispered to her, "Your father is here. He is taking you home. Floodwaters have been rising for the last month because of the constant rain, and your father was afraid if you didn't come on now, you wouldn't be able to make it. The riverbanks are caving in, and the floodwaters are rising and spilling over the lower river basins, so he is here to get you.

"He is?!" Jessica was shocked.

"Yes, he is," Dean Devonshire responded. "He is in the main office, and you will be leaving to go home. Y'all will go to Wilshire Academy and get your belongings, and then you all will be heading back to Staunton."

"Okay, okay," Jessica agreed.

Then Jessica walked over to Anthony, Charles, and Isabella.

"My dad's here to take me home. The constant rain has flooded the Staunton rivers and streams and the riverbanks are caving in. The streams and tributaries are overflowing and covering the roads. My father is afraid if I do not come home now, I will not be able to get in with the floodwaters rising, so I have to say goodbye."

Anthony immediately took Jessica into his arms. "I'm sorry," he said. "I'll contact you in a few days. That is, if the services are available for me to reach you."

"Jessica." Anthony grabbed her and told her, "I love you." And they kissed for the last time.

Then Jessica Leigh was off with Dean Devonshire and Doctor McKinley to the main house to meet her father. The ride from West Virginia University to Wilshire Academy was the longest wagon ride Jessica Leigh had ever experienced. Her father did not say one word to her during the entire drive back to the Academy. Jessica knew her father was troubled and upset, so she didn't say anything herself.

When he pulled up in front of Wilshire Academy, he looked over at her and said, "I'll go with you. You'll need to carry most of your clothes. I do not know when you will be back."

"What do you mean, Father?" She grabbed his arm just patiently waiting for an explanation.

"We had to make temporary arrangements on the plantation," he exclaimed. "The streams and rivers are flooded. If the banks cave in, the main road to Staunton plantation will be covered in water, and the only way will be able to navigate is by boat."

"It's bad, isn't it?" Jessica muttered.

"Yes, it is," he replied. "The rain has finally stopped but now we are having to wait on the South River to crest. Could be several more days, maybe even into next week. Meanwhile, we are having to move everything up to higher ground. Let's go on in and get your things."

Jessica and her father went into the dormitory hall, and walked up to the second floor. As they entered the room, Hortense was startled. She was studying on her bed.

"Well, hello, Mr. Staunton. Surprised to see you here."

"I'm a little early. With the flooding around my area, I wanted to be sure Jessica Leigh could get home in time for the holidays. The river will crest in three or four days. Then it may be too late to make it in. Please help me and Jessica get everything packed to go home."

Hortense got off the bunk and went to the closet. Jessica Leigh put several dresses from the closet into the suitcase.

Jessica said, "Hortense, get those white blouses from

my drawer and put them in the suitcase. Please be sure to include all the undergarments."

"I'll get all my shoes and socks," she muttered as she hurriedly packed the suitcase for travel. After packing the girls, embraced each other.

Then Mr. Staunton said, "We will notify you as soon as we make plans on what we're going to do."

The ride home was very depressing for Jessica and her father. Never before in the history of Staunton Plantation had there ever been a flood so severe and damaging as this one. As Jessica found out when she arrived home, much of the tobacco land had been ruined. The livestock and Appaloosa horses had been moved twenty five miles away. The devastation was unbelievable. The house was still standing, but the floodwaters were well over six feet high on the bottom floor. Most of the workers from Staunton had been moved to Charlottesville, a little larger town east of Staunton. Mr. Carlton and Teddy had some relatives living in Charlottesville, Virginia, and they could use and accommodate the hired help while the floodwater receded.

So, several days after the waters began to rise, the Staunton brothers packed up their people and headed to Charlottesville.

"Ms. Jessie, Ms. Jessie! I am glad you are home!" Rosie hollered with excitement as she saw Jessica Leigh with her father. "I have been praying for you to come home. I knowed you would know what to do, when you got back home."

"Rosie," Jessica explained. "Papa has said very little to me since he picked me up from school, so frankly I do not know what is going on."

"Ms. Jessie, Ms. Jessie, it all has to do with that baby Indian skull," Rosie exclaimed.

Then Jessica Leigh said, "What are you talking about?"

"You 'member, you 'member, Ms. Jessie, you 'member when we was little girls, and the Indian skull talked to us?" Rosie tried to make her remember.

"Are you talking about that baby skull who made us move him to the second floor?" Jessica asked. "Yes, and we put him in this trunk in your baby room."

"Yes, I remember now. Well, what happened?" Jessica quizzed her again.

"Well, we were on the second floor, cleaning the rooms for Ms. Leslie, the lady surveyor," Rosie answered. "Then Samantha was rummaging around the room, and she found the baby's skull that we had put in the trunk years ago."

"I had forgotten all about that skull," Jessica added.

"Well," Rosie continued the story. "We got scared, and I told her to take this baby skull to Alligator Swamp and to dump it back into the swampy waters. We had to give it back to the Indians, before they found out it was out of the grandfather clock."

"Well, what happened?" Jessica asked.

"She lied, Ms. Jessie. She told me she took it back and threw it in the swamp, but she lied," Rosie tried to explain. "She took it to the Negro quarters and hid it under her bed. We was all scared! Colored folks know when the Indians get mad, they cause havoc!"

"So that's what the blackbirds are all about?" Jessica asked. "Yes, ma'am, yes, ma'am. White Feather sent word that the Indians wanted it back in the grandfather clock, but Miss Cadelia couldn't find the key." Rosie was explaining as fast as she could.

"Why didn't you tell her where the key was?" Jessica tried to understand.

"I was scared! I was scared! I didn't say nothing to nobody. I just prayed for you to come home."

"So, what happened next?" Jessica persistently asked.

"Well," Rosie continued. "When we didn't put it back in the clock, Miss Cadelia sent Rooster to White Feather and said we couldn't find the key to unlock the bottom drawer, which was the secret compartment that the skull was to go back in."

Then Jessica remarked, "And that's when the blackbirds came?"

"That's right, the blackbirds started bombarding the countryside looking for the key that went to the secret compartment. The blackbirds broke the windows on the second floor. They stole the key and carried the key to White Feather. Miss Cadelia finally got the key, and put the baby's skull back into the clock. But by then the rains had already come, the rivers and the creeks had already flooded, and the damage was done!"

Then Jessica asked Rosie again, "Why didn't you tell them about the key before it got so bad?"

"Oh, Ms. Jessie – oh, Ms. Jessie," Rosie apologized. "I know what I should've done, but you remember when we was little girls, you knows we promised we would tell nobody about this skull or the key."

"Yes, I remember making that promise. But, Rosie, when the rains came and the twisters came and when the hail came, what did you think?" Jessica asked.

"I didn't think nothing. I was just scared, Ms. Jessie – I was just scared," Rosie admitted. "I didn't know what to do. I wanted you to come home so bad so I could ask you what to do."

"So, where's Miss Cadelia?" Jessica noticed that Miss Cadelia was nowhere in sight.

"Well, when she finally put this skull back into the clock, her heart gave out! Doctor Teddy said her heart just quit working. She can't walk and she can't be no help to Mister Staunton."

"What's going to happen to her?" Jessica gulped with sorrow. "Lordy, Ms. Jessie, I do not know, I really do not know," Rosie exclaimed.

"So, where is everybody?" Jessica inquired. "Your papa sent them all to Charlottesville. He kept just a few of us on – me, Samantha, Cotton, and Rooster. We gonna try to make it 'til the rain waters go down and the roads open up again. Leddy Gail, Miss Cadelia, and Helsinki and the rest of them, plus the youngsters all went to Charlottesville. Your papa sent the boys on out to the Dakotas to get the Appaloosas."

"This is a little early, isn't it?" Jessica asked. "Yes, but it was best! Because there ain't nothing to do around here except wait for the waters to go down."

"So, what do we do now?" Jessica questioned. "Your papa has moved most of the things to the second floor, and we're just waiting till the waters goes down."

CHAPTER 12

The Trail Ride

Nevada and the trail riders were on their way to Colorado Springs to bring back the horses. Carlton had already gotten most of the buyers for the Appaloosas. Now the men had to make the journey out West and bring the horses back to Staunton Plantation.

Nevada was a little puzzled as he explained to the other riders, "Seems rightfully strange for us to be leaving before spring."

Sherwin agreed. "I know what he said, but he ain't been on one of these trail rides since I've been riding with him."

Then Rex interjected. "Me too, how about you, Buck?"

Buck was the oldest of the riders. "Now, let me think," he thought and added, "I do believe Mr. Staunton was with us on one of the first rides. Staunton Plantation had been operating five or so years. We were just starting to invest in the Appaloosas."

"I remember now," he thought. "Mrs. Staunton was pregnant and Carlton was worried. He was afraid he wouldn't make it back for the baby's birth and sure enough he didn't."

"What do you mean?" Rex questioned.

Buck explained, "Well, we were on the way back. We had purchased fifty or so head and were almost home. We were coming through the Wilderness Trail in the Appalachians, when a whirlwind storm blew up. The horses were young, and some of the boys were very inexperienced, so the storm started brewing, and the horses got excited and half the herd got away. It took nearly a full week to recover the horses, and even with our best, we lost a dozen or so of the Appaloosas. Mr. Staunton was new at trail riding himself, and when the herd got into a panic and were running wild, it was chaotic for us. Why, I remember an old cowhand, a likable fella by the name of Broomstick. He was a tall, likeable guy with yellow gold, thick hair. He was a smart fellow though. He seemed to be able to read them horses. Yes, he seemed to have a lot of horse sense about himself. When the horses scattered, he simply calmed Carlton down, by telling him I know where the Appaloosas went and how far away they actually were. Then Broomstick showed us how to read the horses minds: you got to listen to their hooves in the distance."

"How can you read a horse's mind?" Carlton questioned. "I never heard of that kind of mind reading."

Another trail rider responded by saying, "Sounds like bullshit."

"Well," Buck continued the story. "We had a rope. A rock was tied to the rope. He would sling the rock around his head, and when the rock and rope landed, that was the directions the horses had gone. He then would put his ear to the ground. That would tell us how far the horses were from us."

"Bullshit." The other trail riders expressed their opinions of such an asinine thought.

"Well, anyway," Buck vowed for his story. "I can't help what I believe. But the horses had split up. One group of horses went up the river near Goshen Springs, and the others followed the stream south of Silver Rock. When he slung that rope, and he followed the direction of the rock, Broomstick led us to both groups of horses, and we finally made it home, back to Staunton."

"Yep," Buck bragged. "Mr. Carlton knew none of the rest of us could read them horses like Broomstick could, and Mr. Staunton never let us boys leave Staunton Plantation to bring horses back unless Broomstick was at the head of the drive."

Then Roddy spoke up. "I'm not worried about our bringing the horses back — I'm just wondering about the snow and freezing weather with us starting six weeks early we could easily run into snowstorms. We've never left this time of the year."

"Well," Nevada interrupted. "I guess Mr. Staunton didn't have nothing for us to do with the Coon River flooding. There ain't nothing to do but wait for the floodwaters to go down."

"Or," Rex suggested. "Would you have rather joined the rest of the group and gone to Charlottesville to work with Carlton's nephew, while we wait for the waters to go down?"

"No, no, no," Sherwin exclaimed. "This is just as bad a predicament for all of us."

"Well," Rex addressed the matter. "I just hope Mr. Carlton can keep all of us on when we get back."

"Hadn't thought of that," Roddy declared. "Hadn't even crossed my mind about any of us being laid off."

"Lordy," Nevada said. "Guess we all better start praying. If we lose Staunton, we done lost our livelihood."

As the trail riders continued to travel on horseback, Rex observed and spoke up.

"Looks like the sun is going down. Why don't we camp down towards Bear Creek? The horses are tired, and I know you boys are sleepy. We've been riding long before daybreak, and now it's nearly sundown."

Then Roddy suggested, "Why don't you and Nevada get the meal to going, and me and Sherwin will take care of the horses."

Buck added, "Sure thing, boss."

Buck had been the chief cook for the trail riders since he was a kid.

Then Sherwin added, "Josh, why don't you look for a place for us to bed down?"

As Rex looked into the distance, he said, "I hear thunder and see lightning. The lightning is about to strike."

The whole Northeast had been having fast and furious thunderstorms. Flooding had been very prevalent for the past month.

Nevada inquired, "Wonder if the bad weather is occurring all over the country are just in these parts?"

Roddy answered, "Lord, I hope not!"

"I'm sure Carlton was hoping the weather would be drier out West," Sherwin declared.

"Yes." Nevada worried. "I can just see us all drowning in a gully washer!"

"Worst yet," Roddy added. "Imagine us all drowning

after the purchase of the Appaloosas."

"Just pray," Rex begged. "That the rains will stop and we can make the trip."

"Shut up, you guys!" Josh hollered. "We need to get some sleep. It will be daybreak before you know it."

Early the next morning the men were gathering around the covered wagon. Each time they go out West, all of their tools, ammunition, clothing, and medicines, plus any and everything needed for the four-to-six-month journey had been packed. Lanterns, heaters, coal for light and warmth and hay for the horses were packed in the wagons along with water canteens for pure drinking water. All the men were very leery and skeptical. Never before had they left two months early on the trail ride. You have to be careful, when the snow and blizzards start. It is very hard on the Cowboys and the horses. Hopefully – just hopefully – they will be able to make a successful run. Josh and Buck had the breakfast prepared long before the men got up.

The coffee was on the fire, and the flat pan biscuits were cooking. The coffee was perking over the fire and the aroma was strong and filled the whole campsite. Josh rang the breakfast bell, and the men knew it was 4:30 or 5:00 a.m., and the day was about to begin. Sherwin and Rex were the first up. Sherwin was holding his tin cup, heading for the fire where the coffee was brewing. Wearing only his long johns, Sherwin is always the first for his cup of coffee. He usually drinks several cups before the ride starts. Sitting on a large rock, Rex is studying a man-made map for the route to Jefferson City. Josh poured a cup of coffee and scooped up a cup of grits and took it to Rex.

"We gotta detour. Sunshine Valley is flooded, and the

back swamp is too dangerous. Snakes will eat us alive," Rex addressed the problem. "We'll swing back around. Shouldn't set us back but a day or so."

Roddy and the Nevada moseyed on over to the camp-fire. Taking their cups and tin plates, they waited on Josh to serve them.

"Smells mighty good, Buck," Roddy said.

"Thanks, but I know you all really miss Miss Cadelia's biscuits and homemade jam," Buck exclaimed graciously.

"Well," Nevada remarked. "Beggars can't be choosers."

"You're right! We might as well get used to it. Don't look for home-cooked meals till we get to Jefferson City," Roddy said, then continued, "Eat up, men, time to get started!"

Then Josh and Buck began to pick up. Josh knew he was responsible for cleaning up the cooking area. He had to wash the cooking utensils, pots, pans, and dishes. Then the two of them, Buck and Josh, cleaned up the area where they had cooked, and then they had to load the wagon. The horses had to be saddled up and fed. The sleeping gear had to be nicely folded and placed in the back of the wagon. Everything had to be organized, and it had to be placed in an orderly manner, in order for the wagon to hold everything.

Sherwin got on his horse. He was leading the trail ride. The cowboys followed him, and the wagon trailed alone at the end of the train. The sun was brightly shining, and the weather was very pleasant. The men were scattered about' mile apart while on the trail ride. Sherwin always led the ride. Nevada and Roddy rode together most of the time to get the Appaloosas. Josh and Buck traveled with the wagon, and Rex travelled behind. He was always watching for danger, which might pop up at any time. There was always the chance of running into unfriendly Indians or rustlers looking for an easy rob.

The group of men had been working together for about three years. Most of the trail rides had been pretty successful. Sherwin and Rex had been with Mr. Staunton for well over ten years, so their expertise was invaluable. Nevada and Roddy had been on the trail rides for five or six years. Josh was the newcomer. He had been with the group less than a year, and of course Buck, the cook, was as old as the hills.

"You gotta talk to those men about bathing," Sherwin fussed.

"I guess they have grown accustomed to the odor," Rex observed.

"Well, with me riding ahead, I don't notice it, but when we meet back day or night, I can hardly stand to be near any of them," Sherwin added. "And tell Roddy to throw those dang jeans away — I don't think those fumes can ever come out of his trousers."

"Sure thing," Rex interjected.

"Next stop is near Sandy Cove. There is a lake nearby, and that would be a perfect place to skinny-dip and rid ourselves of this stench," Sherwin ordered. "Oh, by the way, just tell those fellows to stay away from me. I swear, the boys smell like a pack of skunks."

Later, the men are all bathing in Fenn Lake. Their clothes were hanging on the nearby trees, airing out. Buck is at the stove preparing for the night meal. Rex had cut the trail ride short, because Fenn Lake was very near Sandy Cove, and that's where the men were going to camp for a night or so.

The next part of the journey would take the men through Wilderness Trail. This would be a long stretch, and this may be the only chance the man had to bathe before the ride through Wilderness Trail began. So, needless to say, Rex decided to take advantage of this much-needed event before the long ride started through Wilderness Trail. The trail would take the Cowboys through the Appalachian Mountains. The men were enjoying the cool water; washing, playing, and cutting up. The naked men were a little cool, because the stream ran right out of the mountains into the little lake and on southward. The water was cool mountain water.

The men stripped out of all their clothing, and all of them were rustling and tussling in the lake near the campsite. Supposedly, the men were bathing because they had not bathed since the beginning of the journey. Rex had stressed all of the them to rub and scrub until all the dirt and odor was gone. Buck is at the fire preparing for the afternoon meal. Rick said cut the trail ride short, because they were going to reach Wilderness Road within the next ten hours, and there would not be another opportunity to relax and bathe before the long ride through the Appalachian Mountains. So, Rex had decided to take this opportunity for the Cowboys. They were all enjoying the afternoon wash. All of them was as naked as could be, and they were enjoying the cool stream.

Every chance they got, Roddy and Nevada would get together, tackle Rex and hold him down under the water as long as they could. It didn't seem to matter though, because Rex was stronger than Roddy and Nevada together. Age didn't seem to matter much. Rex was just a strong guy.

Sherwin was having the most fun. There was an old tree branch which had been broken off from the main trunk of the tree, and Sherwin was using it as a diving board. He had done a couple of jackknives, then a belly buster -a cannonball. The old branch made an excellent diving board.

Then Rex hollered, "Use that soap – we didn't stop here to just have fun. Miss Cadelia sent plenty of soap. She knew we would stink to high heaven, if we didn't do something to get rid of the smell."

However, the men continued to frolic in the water. The food was smelling good. Several hours before the Cowboys had cut the brush and grass, making a perfect campsite. Rex had planned to stay here for two nights, because it was a long and exhausting journey through the Cumberland Gap. So, everyone was relaxed, not anticipating any danger or troubles. Buck was preparing a specialty for the men: salt meat from the smokehouse back home and fried trout. Buck rigged up his fishing pole while the men were bathing, and he snagged two nice sized trout. He put the dried purple hull peas on the fire along with the fried hoe cakes. Then to top the meal off, Miss Cadelia had packed dried peaches and apples. All Buck had to do was put them in water over a fire, and leave them boil. Yes, the men were looking forward to a nice delicious meal, and since Rex had planned to stay two nights, the tents had been put up, and the men were really beginning to relax. They were looking forward to the next two days.

The two-day break was gladly appreciated. The men had been riding straight without a break since they left Staunton Plantation. The Wilderness Road would be a two-hundred-mile stretch, riding through the mountains and on into Kentucky. So, Rex had planned a two-day resting stop at the right time. Roddy and Nevada were really having fun. As they came up for air, they glanced toward the riverbank, and they became startled. "What's wrong?" Sherwin hollered as he looked toward the riverbank. The men were all shocked and frightened. There were four Shawnee Indians on horseback facing the river. Then there were another two Indians standing on the ground. The last Indian was standing near Buck with a rifle pointed toward his head. The one who held the rifle said something to Buck, and Buck hollered to the naked men in the stream.

"Get your clothes on. They want to talk."

In the years past, it was very dangerous to travel on The Wilderness Trail, better known as the Cumberland Gap. The Shawnee and Cherokee Indians had killed over 100 travelers. Rex had not been too worried. He figured that an Indian attack would not take place until they were well into the Wilderness Trail. So needless to say, Rex was quite shocked to see the Indians so near the Tennessee line. The four naked men climbed out of the water and slipped into their clothes. As they walked toward the campfire, the other four Indians got off their horses and pointed their guns toward the men. Yes, the trail riders were scared, caught off guard and empty handed. When the men got on the shore and closer to the campsite, the men found out that the Indian who had pointed the gun toward Buck was the leader of the group. He could speak English quite well, along with his Shawnee. He spoke English to the Cowboys, and then spoke Shawnee to the Indians.

The leader spoke to the Cowboys, "We want no trouble. We just want your horses and supplies and we will give you your life."

Then Rex walked toward the leader and said, "We could be here for days, even weeks."

The leader replied, "Probably in a week or so. Pioneers will come through every few weeks, so you'll just have to make do with what you've got."

Then the leader spoke to his Shawnee tribesmen, and told them to get the covered wagon and all the supplies and the horses.

"The hell you say," Roddy blurted out. With a loaded pistol in his trousers, he pulled it out and pulled the trigger.

Chi Howie fell to the ground with a bullet lodged somewhere under his shoulder blade. Then the commotion began. All the Cowboys hit the ground as the rifle started firing. Again, Rex stepped forward, and bent down on the ground next to Chi Howie.

"Tell your men to stop firing. I can take the bullet out and clean up your injury. Then you all can take all our things and go. We don't want any more bloodshed."

The old leader, Chi Howie, gave the instructions to his Indians. The Indians must've been

satisfied, because they gathered up the Cowboys and tied them up Indian style. The Indians drove a stake in the ground and drove five smaller stakes around the large one in the middle. They had the Cowboys lay on the ground. They bound their legs in their hands together. Each cowboy was tied to one of the small stakes. Then the Indians waited on new instructions from Chi Howie.

Meanwhile Rex laid Chi Howie comfortably down on a blanket. Two Indians were standing on each side of Rex and Chi Howie. The rifles were pointed at Rex the entire time that the procedure was done. Rex inspected the gunshot wound.

Then Rex told the leader, "Tell your men I've got to get the medicine out of the wagon. I will have to sterilize the knife, then I'll remove the bullet."

In a low whisper, Chi Howie related the message to the men.

Then Rex said, "I've got to hurry. You're losing a lot of blood."

Rex headed toward the covered wagon with two Indians by his side and rifles aimed at his head. He climbed into the wagon and quickly came out with the black medicine bag. The medical bag had belonged to Doctor Teddy Staunton years ago, when he was in medical school. However, when he got into private practice, Carlton suggested that the trail riders take it with them on each trip out West to get the Appaloosas. Dr. Staunton had carefully prepared Rex on taking care of simple wounds which might occur on the trail rides. Snakebite injuries, broken limbs, flu and pneumonia illnesses had been discussed at great length. As a matter of fact, Rex had even observed Dr. Staunton during several surgeries, while he removed bullets from a gunshot wound and stitching up the hole in the patient's skin. So, Rex was very prepared and knowledgeable on how to remove the bullet that Chi Howie had in his body.

When Rex returned to Chi Howie, he also had a jug of distilled whiskey. He told Chi Howie, "Drink as much as you can so you won't feel the pain."

Chi Howie took the jug and slowly drank most of the whiskey, then he passed out. Rex didn't know whether he passed out because he was drunk or because the pain was so extreme. Regardless, Rex was glad that he had passed out, because now Rex could begin to operate. The strategic plan was to enter the skin one inch from the bullet wound and remove the bullet and pull the metal from the flesh through the incision. He would remove the bullet through the 1-inch incision. This way the flesh would not be further destroyed, and it would be easier to sew up. The surgery lasted a little over two hours. Rex removed the bullet and sewed up the skin. Thank goodness, the bullet did not cause any damage to the arteries or veins. The bullet was not very deep.

Then Rex motioned to the Indians on each side where Chi Howie needed to lay down in order to sleep. Rex then went over to a large rock, sat down, and leaned against the rock. By the time Rex sat down to rest, one of the Indians motioned for Rex to put his hands behind his back, and the Indians tied his hands and feet with rope. Rex thought this will probably be a long night. The rest of the trail riders were about ten yards away from the campsite. The Indians had tied the Cowboys up Shawnee style. Each man was laying on the ground, hands and feet bound with rope. The men were in a circle, one stake in the middle of the ground with five smaller stakes forming the circle. The men were tied to the stake next to them with their hands and feet bound. The tallest stake in the middle was about five feet high, while the smaller stakes were about three feet high. The guns were all pointed toward Rex.

The Indians began to communicate with each other. Then in sign language, they nudged him with their guns. After the Indians cut his hands loose, Rex went toward the campsite got the tin plates and served the Indians the food which was warming on the fire. The Indians had motioned with their hands that they wanted to eat the food from the fire kettle. Then they tied Rex back up, and he wondered what would happen next.

Several hours had passed. There was no mention of feeding the Cowboys. Night had fallen, and the Indians had found themselves a place to sleep. At this time, there was only one Indian standing guard.

"What's gonna happen to us?" Roddy said.

"Beats me," Nevada answered.

"I'm surprised they just didn't kill us on the spot," Roddy responded.

"I don't think they wanted to start any trouble. I honestly believe they just wanted to steal our supplies and horses." Nevada was hoping for reassurance.

"Yeah, wonder if Chi Howie will make it?" Roddy asked.

"I sure hope he does. He is our only hope." Nevada declared.

The men tried to sleep. Their bodies would lean and fall over, as they tried to get some sleep. The cowboys had been dozing on and off for several hours to get some sleep. Around 3 a.m., there was a commotion in the brush. The voices of the Indians were getting louder and louder. You could hear the Indians rustling around the brush. Definitely the Indians were disturbed about something. The cowboys were all wide awake by now, just wondering and waiting for what was going to happen next.

"What's happening?" Buck asked.

"I don't know," Josh said as he looked around.

"But they do seem upset, don't they?" Buck muttered.

Josh broke in. "Well, we know we haven't done anything.

We can't even move with these ropes strung all over us."

The Indians were awfully upset. Five of the Indians came toward the cowboys, and they were very confused. They had bridled one of the Appaloosas, and the Indians were leading the pony toward the Cowboys.

"What are they doing?"

Then one of the Indians took the Philly, raised her tail toward the left side and indicated a mark on her leg. The brand looked like a broken ring or circle. There was a squiggly line resembling a backwards S drawn through the broken band. Then the Indians began to talk back and forth in their Shawnee language. They began to holler and holler and scream- getting louder and louder.

"What are they talking about?" Rex questioned.

"Beats me…beats me," Sherwin muttered.

Two of the Indians went over to Chi Howie, hovering over him, they began to try to wake him up.

"Ugh, ugh…" Chi Howie rolled over and struggled to wake up. Then the two Indians began rattling in their native language, while they were pointing to the mark on the Appaloosa pony. Slowly, Chi Howie turned over and looked straight into the Indians eyes. Shocked, he responded in Shawnee language. The Indians talked several minutes to each other. Hearing all the commotion, Rex began to call to Chi Howie.

He called over and over and finally Chi Howie responded. Talking in Shawnee, he gave his instructions to have Rex brought to him. The Indians went over and brought him back to Chi Howie. They released the rope from his hands and feet. Then the Indians proceeded to lean Chi Howie up next to a tree. Using a blanket as a pillow, they tried to make their leader as comfortable as possible. Chi Howie motioned for Rex to lean down toward him. He was very weak and did not have much strength to talk. Chi Howie started the conversation. His main concern was about the brand on the Appaloosa pony.

"My people do not understand the brand on this pony. It troubles them greatly, the broken band and the squiggly line. Look at her brand and tell me what it means to your people," Chi Howie demanded an answer.

Rex was very relieved when he understood the situation. "Here, let me explain it to you, Chi Howie!" Rex exclaimed. "The broken band, as you call it, stands for Carlton, and the squiggly line drawn down the middle stands for Staunton. Carlton Staunton is the name of our herd."

Then Rex took a stick and drew letters on the ground.

He said, "This type of brand is not uncommon. All of our cattle and horses are branded with the C and S burned on the animal. The S overlaps the C like this."

Then Chi Howie became frustrated and tired from trying to explain himself, and he passed out. Then the two Indians who brought the pony over began to shake their heads no, no, no.

Rex then took his stick and drew the brand emblem on the ground for the two Indians to see for themselves. One of the Indians grabbed the stick and drew the sign on the ground and shook his head and said something that meant, "no, no, no, no."

Then he drew another emblem that was identical to the one which was burned on the pony. It was a C with a backwards S, and both letters were the same size.

"Oh, I see."

Then the Indians moved the tail over to indicate the brand on the pony was different from the rest of the Appaloosas.

Well, Rex thought, I don't know.

The tied-up cowboys began to holler.

"What's that all about?" Roddy hollered.

"What's up?" Josh screamed.

"What's happening?" Buck asked in a startled tone.

One of the Indians began to shake Chi Howie again. The Indian kept punching Chi Howie and saying, "ish no, ish no," meaning tell the story to the men. He's got to know the truth.

Chi Howie rolled over again and tried to explain to Rex what this was all about. In his weak voice, he tried to explain the situation, "M. Shay, an Indian princess, had a baby papoose. He died when he was only a few weeks old. His skull was hidden in an old grandfather clock on Staunton Plantation. Our Native American customs regarding life after death are very spiritual. M. Shea was a great Shawnee Indian princess. She disobeyed her father by marrying a British commander, and when her first child was born — the child was cursed. He could not move his arms or legs. He died when he was three weeks old. M. Shay knew there was only one way her son could return to his afterlife. His tiny skull would have to be placed in hidden in a secret compartment of a grandfather clock. Then when he was born again — he would return as a noble man, and his responsible duty would be to return all lands that the white man had stolen from the Indians back to the red man. The white men and government had stolen the lands from the Indian tribes in America years earlier."

"Why?" Rex asked. "Did M. Shay choose Staunton Plantation?"

Chi Howie answered, "Because the old Shawnee burial ground were located just five miles to the north of Staunton, Virginia. Over the years the burial grounds flooded, and the area became swamplands."

"But," Rex asked again. "Why did she choose Staunton?"

Chi Howie continued the legend, "Her spiritual ancestors instructed her where the skull was to be hidden. The plantation was not built at that particular time, but the Indian spirits could see the future. So, following their instructions, the Indians spirits made arrangements for the skull to be placed and locked in a secret compartment of the grandfather clock on Staunton Plantation. The old clock has purposeful powers. The old clock knew the exact year, the exact time, and the exact date and place of the baby's new arrival birth. All the Indians, buried behind Staunton Plantation, also knew the same information. The grandfather clock related the information to the ancestral spirits, and they shared the information when they would return to the old lagoon. So, all the Shawnee tribes have been anxiously awaiting for the birth of the new baby with exhilaration."

Then Rex looked dumbfounded. He questioned, "How can a clock tell you anything? A clock is made of lumber, metal, copper, and screws. How can a clock reveal anything about human encounters?"

Then Chi Howie answered Rex, "The Shawnee Indians believe the white man's tall clock can transfer a Shawnee spirit to the next world."

"What do you mean to the Next World?" Rex questioned.

"Well, the Indians spirit will actually be reborn into another family. The clock will designate the exact time, date, and the year that the transfer will take place. M Shay preplanned, and she had the baby's skull place in the white man's house on Staunton Plantation."

"So," Rex questioned again. "What is a concern about the brand on the Appaloosa pony?"

Rex then drew the brand on the ground again. "Why is this sign so important?"

Chi Howie tried to explain. "The broken ring, which looks like a broken circle, means that a band of Shawnee Indians broke off from the Cherokee tribe. Our Indian heritage tells us that one day a child will reunite the Cherokee and Shawnee, and the child would be of noble heritage and he would be influential in returning all the rightful lands back to the Native American tribes throughout America."

"Well," Rex interrupted, "What about the squiggly line drawn through the broken band?"

"That's where the mystical spirits took over," the old Indian replied.

"What do you mean took over?" Rex quizzed him again. "We believe our ancestors are still with us here on earth as well as being in a heavenly form, but they only take on human activity when they are on a mission to help us, when we are in danger. They return to our vision and render the service needed at that time. Then they return to the heavenly bodies with the rest of our ancestors."

"So, what about the squiggly line?" Rex still asked.

"The squiggly line drawn through the band stands for Staunton Plantation," Chi Howie answered.

"What?" Rex hollered. "What do you mean?"

Chi Howie continued, "M. Shay had a baby skull placed in the tall clock on Staunton Plantation. The skull was placed in the secret locked drawer at the base of the clock. The ancestral spirits branded the baby pony with the sign. The pony was branded right after the baby was born. When the baby died, the old Indian custom was to break the pony's neck, and the two were buried together at the old Indian burial ground."

"Why did the Indians kill the pony anyway?" Rex questioned.

"Indian custom says that when the baby skull is about to be reborn the baby Appaloosa will miraculously appear, getting ready for the arrival of the new leader for the Indians," Chi Howie explained, then continued, "Our people have no Arabic letters, but the spirits instructed them to brand the squiggly line over the broken band."

"Which…" Rex interrupted. "When reversed, the squiggly line resembled the letter S, which stands for Staunton, and the broken band stands for Carlton."

"Right," Chi Howie agreed. "Then the baby is scheduled at a precise day, year, and time to be reborn on Staunton Plantation. He will be the leader of the American nation and bring the justice and reconciliation back to the American Native Indians. The injustice that the red man endured when the white man arrived on our native soil and stole the land from us."

Then Rex asked, "So, what about this pony, and how long will we live?"

Chi Howie replied, "The pony will not die until the baby is grown, and the two of them ride together, renewing and unifying all Native Americans from the injustices imposed on them by the white man."

"Unbelievable," Rex said. It's hard for me to understand this story, much less believe it."

"It doesn't matter!" Chi Howie exclaimed. "My Shawnee people are well aware that the white men from Staunton Plantation are sacred to our people, and we will provide protection for your men for the rest of the journey through the Appalachian Mountains and back home."

"Now, please," Chi Howie begged. "Allow me to sleep."

Next, Chi Howie motioned for the two men to come to him. He gave them instructions to cut the men apart from the sticks and wait outside the campsite. He also explained in detail that the Shawnee would escort the Cowboys through the Wilderness Trail and escort them back when they return with the Appaloosas; they would escort them back through the gap. The Indians would provide the protection the men from Staunton needed as they traveled back through the Cumberland Gap. Truly the Shawnee regarded the Staunton family as sacred people.

At last, the cowboys had made the trip through the Wilderness Road. The trip was relatively easy, considering all the troubles they had with Chi Howie and his band of Indians – and yes, the Indians led, directed, and protected the men from Staunton Plantation, as they traveled through the sixty-mile gap between the Appalachian Mountains. As they parted ways, Rex and his men thanked the Shawnees for all that they had done for them. The magnificent story of the Indian skull, placed on Staunton Plantation, was almost unbelievable. The Cowboys would carry this Indian tale to their graves. Now, whether the Cowboys actually believed the story is yet to be told. But Chi Howie and his tribe had no reservations. They knew when they saw the Appaloosa pony, branded with the squiggly line through the broken circle, that the promised one would be born on the plantation. It would probably be during their lifetime, because when the pony appeared, that was the prophecy that the little one was soon to be born to redeem their people.

The long journey began. The Cowboys knew that they would be riding a long drive, because they would not be stopping until they reached Jefferson City, Missouri. The snow began fall. The cold eastern winds were bringing in hail, along with the light snow patches. The men were tired, and they knew the remainder of the journey would be rough. They would ride as long as they could. Then they would have to finish early in order to set up the campsite. With the wood burning and a fire in each tent was the only way the men could make it through the night. You could hear the wind howling, as it rustled through the trees, with rain and sleet peppering

down. Crackling branches would screech as the limbs fell to the ground. Getting to bed early each night was a must. The men needed at least four to five hours of sleep before waking up and starting back on the cold, long journey.

Before daybreak, Buck would have the breakfast on the fire. The coffee was brewing, and the men were scurrying to start the day's journey. Six weeks had passed, since they left the Cumberland Gap. Rex, Sherwin, and Buck were up especially early this morning.

Sherwin was speculating. "Think we will make it to Jefferson City by the end of the week?"

"Probably so," Rex replied. "I'm pleased that the snow has not bogged us down any more than it has."

"I figured it would have been worse than this," Rex declared. "I was really dreading starting the trail ride five weeks early."

Then Buck broke in. "Guess the late frost has helped us out."

"I certainly hope so," Roddy exclaimed. "But, as you all recall, last year that storm from the West Coast set us back two extra weeks."

"Oh, yeah," Sherwin remembered. "I'd forgotten about that."

"I have not forgotten it," Roddy announced. "That's when I came down with the flu and almost died."

Rex assured Roddy, "You didn't almost die. We had it well under control. It just set you under the weather for several days."

Then Buck advised, "We best get the men up and get started."

Buck rang the breakfast bell, and the rest of the cowboys joined the group.

They traveled over the horizon. You could see the bustling cowboy town of Jefferson City, Missouri. The Main Street was busy with lots of activity. The old General Store had polished oak counters and vintage display cases. Fabrics of all kinds had been shipped from the east. Tobacco tins and wooden barrels surrounded the floor with staple foods of all kinds. All the products were available for the surrounding customers and farmers. Some even rode thirty five to forty miles to get their yearly supplies. Shelves were lined with tooth, foot, face, and talcum powders.

Lithograph trays and ledger markers lined the walls. It was a real treat for the customers, when they came to Jefferson City for a buying spree. Next you see the Jefferson City bank. Several houses stood between the bank and the doctor's office. Jefferson City was right proud to have a local doctor and a small infirmary. But when the Cowboys came to town, believe me, the first thing they planned to do was to visit The Blue Dog Saloon. It is an elegant old barroom with blue velvet curtains and stained-glass windows. The circular bar wound around the room, and the spiral staircase went to the second floor. The ladies who danced at The Blue Dog lived on the second floor. The ladies did floor shows, and the shows went on daily. The floor shows were very enticing to encourage nightly visits with the cowboys.

When the cowboys, who had been on the trail rides for months, see The Blue Dog Saloon, their blood sugar began to rise. Nothing beats good old whiskey with a barmaid by your side. The men knew they would first have to go to Mabel's Rooming House. They had been staying there since the trail ride began. Miss Mabel had the best cooking this side of the Mississippi, and she always saved a place for her Staunton boys. At least once a year, the boys would come through Jefferson City traveling to Colorado to get the Appaloosas. As a matter of fact, several years ago, the boys made two trail rides in one year. The boardinghouse was several miles outside of Jefferson City. The Cowboys had to travel through Jefferson City to get to Mabel's Boarding House.

As the group rode through Jefferson City, the whole town knew they had come through again. The townspeople really liked the men from Staunton, Virginia. All the men were very respectable, likable, and hard-working. Jefferson City saw its share of rousters and wranglers barreling through with gun slinging and whiskey drinking on their minds. They had drinking and women on their minds. They brought the money. The turmoil they caused far outweighed the income they brought to town. The townspeople, just as soon as these rousters and wranglers enter, would stay away. As the men got near the boardinghouse, Mr. Gus greeted them at the stable. Mr. Gus oversaw the horses, and he knew the cowboys would be here for several days. The horses need to be fitted with new horseshoes. They need to be fed, and the local vet would need to take a look at each horse. On a trail ride, it is crucial that the riding animals are in good physical condition. These long trips can wear a horse down, and you cannot afford to be caught off guard with a lame animal. Time and money is too valuable to not have the horses properly taken care of.

Mr. Gus greets the boys and said, "Miss Mabel is expecting you all and says she's got the rooms all ready, and the water is being heated for a hot bath." Roddy and Nevada scrambled to see just who will be the first to get in the hot bathtub. Lord only knows, both men need to be scrubbed down before they go inside. They cannot go into town without a bath, even The Blue Dog Saloon is particular about stinking cowboys coming into the saloon. Rex says to Mister Gus, "Check my horse - I'm pretty sure his shoe is loose." Sherwin, Josh, and Buck walk on the to the boarding house. The old white house was very well built. Miss Mabel had 10 rooms. She had a large kitchen and a hot room for bathing. The old house had a large living room and an open parlor. The cowboys were not allowed in the living room/parlor until they were cleaned up.

Miss Mabel had laid down the law. Cleanliness is next to godliness and makes a wholesome cowboy. Miss Mabel met them at the door with clean towels. Rex took the stack of towels, and the men went into the hot room. There were three tubs with hot water bubbling in each tub.

"My! My! My! You fellas need a good scrubbing down," Abby declared.

"Oh, Ms. Abby, we ain't that bad," Rex responded.

"Bad ain't the word, Mr. Rex, it is horrific," she assured him. "I knowed when you fellas rode into town, we had best start steaming the tubs, and I told Miss Mabel to get the soap out cause you fellas hadn't bathed since your last visit to Jefferson City."

"And you are right," Buck agreed. "We ain't tub-bathed since the last time we was through. We did wash the stink off our bodies in the mountain stream on the other side of the mountain."

Mr. Mark, an old black gentleman, came in to assist the men while bathing. Mr. Mark was well into his fifties. He had been with Miss Mabel since he was a little boy. Mr. Mark had a slight limp. When he was young he was injured and never went to the doctor. Miss Abby, a black girl, left the soap with them, and she went on back to the main house to help Miss Mabel in the kitchen. Miss Abby was in her late twenties. Her Pa, Mr. Gus, had been with Miss Mabel ever since she opened the inn. So, as you can see, coming to Miss Mabel's boarding house during the trail ride is very much of a family affair. The cowboys had been staying at Miss Mable's boardinghouse for quite a long while, and they always enjoyed their stay.

"Get in here, Abby!" Miss Mable directed. "The cornbread is done. Take it out of the oven."

"The corn beef hash needs to be checked, and don't forget those roasting ears," she added.

"Yes ma'am," Abby replied.

"Oh, Abby," Miss Mable requested. "When you see your Pa tonight, tell him to check with me early in the morning. Some of the livestock supplies have arrived. Dave sent word that he was waiting on your Pa to pick them up. Several ranchers from North Ranch Road had been inquiring about the supplies, so tell him to check with me in the morning. We need to pick the supplies up pronto!"

"Yes ma'am." Abby replied. "Pa has been wondering why the order had taken so long."

"Well," Miss Mable responded. "Cross River flooded from the last rain, and they have just now repaired the overhead bridge. Dave said it has put several ranchers in a bind."

By the time Miss Abby finished setting the table, the Staunton boys finally approached the kitchen steps.

"You ready for us, Miss Mable?" Rex called.

"You boys, come on in," she announced.

The cowboys hurried into the kitchen and found their seats around the table.

"You boys hungry?" Miss Mable asked.

"You don't know how hungry we are," one of the cowboys spoke up.

"Good," Miss Mable exclaimed. "The food is piping hot and ready to serve."

Miss Mable and Miss Abby served the meal.

As several of the boys started to dig in, Miss Mable

reminded the boys, "Watch your manners! You know Lord God Almighty expects grace before we partake of the good food."

The three men, who had begun filling their plates, stopped immediately. All the other cowboys stared at them unmercifully.

"Rex," Miss Mable asked. "Why don't you say grace?" Rex stood up and thanked the Lord for the safe trip thus far. Rex again asked the Lord for protection for the remainder of the trip.

The men ended the prayer with all cowboys saying, "Amen."

"Gentlemen," Miss Mable announced. "After dinner if you would like, you could join us in the parlor for homemade peach pie and coffee. Otherwise, we'll see you all at 6 a.m. sharp for breakfast."

The men thanked Miss Mable for the meal and the hospitality.

Then Sherwin said, "I think we're all going into town. The boys are eager to visit The Blue Dog Saloon."

"I expected so." Miss Mable chuckled to herself.

Then Rex said, "I'd really prefer relaxing in the parlor with the peach pie and the coffee, but—"

Sherwin interrupted. "Yes, but I figure both of us had best head into town with the boys."

Rex then added, "Want to be sure they don't get into trouble the first night we here in Jefferson City."

By the time Rex and Sherwin left the table, the other three cowboys had already left the table and gotten their horses saddled to go.

"Buck?" Rex questioned. "You're going with us, aren't

you?"

Buck answered, "Not tonight, Rex. I think I'm going to bed early. You know I'm twenty years older than you boys."

"But," Rex replied. "You can run circles around us."

"Well," he said again. "Not tonight – not tonight."

"Goodnight, Buck," Rex added. "Goodnight, Miss Mable. We will see you in the morning."

Buck headed out of the kitchen and on to the second floor. He and Roddy would be sleeping in the second room from the end. He and Roddy would be rooming together for the next two days. As the five men were riding into town, the younger men were all excited.

"You sho' slicked up and looking good," Josh announced.

"As good as I could get for a rusty cowboy," Roddy answered.

"Besides, I ain't looking for no woman. I got my money tied up in playing poker and for a bourbon and tonic all night long."

"You better watch yourself, lose all your money tonight, and you will be drinking coffee and eating pie with Miss Mable tomorrow night," Rex teased.

"I ain't gonna lose," Roddy bragged.

Roddy and Nevada had been practicing for the past several months.

Roddy said, "I am a guaranteed winner in five card stud."

Nevada spoke up. "That's because I let you win. It was easier to give in rather than to listen to you fuss."

Josh then spoke up. "Well, I got a little extra money. Been saving it all year long. Rex, what do you think my best chances are…which table?"

Rex answered, "Well, you might start at the roulette

table. But don't bet too much. Wait and see how you are doing before you go all in."

As they rode closer to town, Rex asked Nevada, "You still got an inkling to see that little gal you were involved with last year?"

Nevada responded, "Probably not — I don't think she appreciated me the last time I was through."

"What really happened?" Sherwin asked. "I've forgotten, except I do remember that she took you for a cleaning, and then she got hitched up with a gunslinger from Kansas City."

"You got most of it right," Nevada answered. "Her gunslinger cornered me in the Blue Dog and threatened to put a bullet in my skull, so I backed off. Ain't no woman worth me losing my life."

"You are speaking the truth," Rex interjected. "The God-fearing truth. Ain't no dance hall girl from Jefferson City worth your time — must less losing your life."

The Staunton boys turned the corner on to Main Street — you could tell excitement was in the air. You could hear the loud noises coming from The Blue Dog Saloon. Flashing blue lights were glittering off and on, and there was hollering and carrying on inside The Blue Dog Saloon. You could tell the men inside the saloon were having a hell of a good time. There was an enormous amount of whiskey flowing inside. The band was playing, and there was dancing on the saloon floor.

"Paradise!" Roddy exclaimed as he and Nevada and Josh opened the saloon doors to all the excitement inside.

"Lord," Josh exclaimed.

Somebody must have robbed a bank with all that money

and poker chips on the gambling tables.

"Yes," Josh thought to himself. "We must be in paradise."

Rex and Sherwin were behind. They wanted to be sure the horses were okay. In this type of town, rustlers are capable of stealing anything, including your horse and saddle. There was a stable two blocks away. Rex talked to the stable hand, and the five horses were boarded at the city stable. Then Rex and Sherwin went on toward the Blue Dog. Once inside, the activity was booming. There were five or six tables in the room. Each table was very involved with gaming activities. There were dozens of customers seated around the circular bar, and many standing while drinking, and many were indulging happily at the bar, gulping down each drink and quickly asking for a refill. Rex and Sherwin quickly decided they would try a little poker. Five card draw was their game. Josh did as suggested and joined in at the roulette table. Roddy and Nevada headed for the circular bar.

Roddy didn't stay long. One of the can-can dancers quickly got his attention, and he went with her upstairs. While sitting at the bar, Nevada first asked for a whiskey sour to wet his windpipe.

Looking all around the room, the can-can dancers were in full swing. There was an elevated dance floor in the right corner of the big room. Several girls were doing their stuff, shaking their fannies and lifting up their petticoat dresses, while the men actually gazed at their lacy panties. The men were hollering, clapping, and trying to entice their chosen girls to notice them. The girls pretty well size up these men before they go upstairs. The girls can pretty well tell which Cowboys have money, and which Cowboys are willing to spend It on them. Looks and age do have some bearing on the situation, but money takes all priority. Prostitution has been in existence in Jefferson City from the time of pioneer days. The only difference is the girls look better – they expect more money – and the girls demand respect from the customers.

The Blue Dog Saloon belonged to Miss Caroline. She was an elderly lady with bleached blonde hair in her fifties. She won The Blue Dog in the street gunfight. She had been a can-can dancer for years. A new marshal came to town about ten years ago. The marshal was sent to the town to straighten up the town from all the riffraff and corruption. The original owner of The Blue Dog and some of his men propositioned the marshal to a duel.

The marshal said, "Okay, if I win you fellows have to leave town, and Miss Caroline becomes the new owner."

"Certainly," the corrupt owner agreed. He figured with five gunslingers against the marshal, what better odds than that? The original owner would certainly win.

When the duel began, two of the gunslingers were immediately killed when the huge glass chandelier miraculously fell right on top of their heads. Two of the owner's men were killed. Miss Caroline was hiding behind the bar with a butcher knife, and she stabbed another man from behind and killed him instantly. The marshal killed the remaining two men with one bullet. The one bullet went through the gunslinger's heart, came out on the other side and hit a large steel horseshoe hanging over the bar. When the horseshoe fell, it knocked the last gunslingers head right off the shoulders. This story may sound unbelievable, but that's the story that all the residents of Jefferson City swear by to be the truth to this day.

Miss Caroline is a nice, honest lady, and she owns half of the town, and the marshal owns the other half.

Then the bartender asked, "You still want another whiskey sour?"

Nevada answered, "No, just give me a brandy, and give me some information. Tell me, I know a woman who was here last year. She had a small body frame, and she had long dark brown hair. I can't remember her name. They just called her Miss G."

"Well, son," the bartender interrupted. "She doesn't work here anymore."

"Well," Nevada questioned. "Has she left town?"

"I can't rightfully tell you that," he answered. "But you might ask Miss Caroline. We're not supposed to give out information about any of the girls who worked here. But Miss Caroline might know of her."

At that Nevada left the bar and moseyed over to the card table, still wondering what happened to Miss G.

"Got room for another?" Nevada inquired.

"Yes, sir," the dealer said. "Just ante up."

The night was young, and enthusiasm ran high.

"What are you playing, Doc?" Nevada asked the dealer.

"Five Card Stud, son."

At that, Nevada began to fidget with his money.

"I'll go too."

The man to the left put his bet in, and all around the table the men responded according to the cards they had in their hand and to the cards shown upright on the table. Nevada took a sip of his drink and got ready to make his second call.

Looking at his hand and the table, he said, "I had better fold."

"Fold!" one man hollered. "You just got in, son!"

"Well," Nevada answered. "I'll quit while I am ahead."

Staring at the winding staircase, Nevada figured the woman coming down the staircase was Miss Caroline. She was an elderly woman, very precise and dignified, and she had blonde hair pulled up in a bun on top of her head. He sort of remembered her from last year.

Nevada got up from the table and inched his way toward the staircase, as the elderly lady was coming down.

"Miss Caroline," Nevada spoke as he approached her.

"Yes, I am Miss Caroline," she replied.

"I'm Nevada Granger from Staunton Plantation out east. If you wouldn't mind, I'd like to buy you a drink. I recognize you from some of my past trips through, and I would like to ask you a few questions. That is, if you don't mind."

"No, I don't mind, cowboy. Let me take care of a little business first. Why don't you tell Jed, the bartender, to take you to my office? I will be there shortly."

Nevada went to the bartender and gave him the message from Ms. Caroline. The two of them went to Miss Caroline's office, which was to the left, behind the winding bar. Jed told Nevada to take a seat, and Miss Caroline would soon be with him. The office was exquisitely decorated. The mahogany stained wood was sanded and polished to perfection. The office was small, however a small chandelier hung in the middle of the room with a cherry chair on each side facing the desk. The large wing chairs were a triangle to the side of the large portrait which was hanging on the wall. The portrait was Miss Caroline. She appeared to be much younger, but the resemblance was obvious. It was Miss Caroline. She was very beautiful with golden hair streaming down her shoulders. Her shadowed blue eyes glistened from the portrait. The painting was made in younger days, but age is not hindered her beauty.

As he was admiring the portrait, Miss Caroline quietly slipped into the room and eased up behind the desk and eased into the chair.

"Now, cowboy," she said. "What can I do for you?"

"Well," he responded. "I'm really looking for someone."

"A lady, I would imagine?" she questioned.

"Yes ma'am, Miss Caroline," Nevada said, continuing, "There was a chorus girl employed here at The Blue Dog. I've been coming to Jefferson City quite a number of years. The young lady I'm inquiring about was called Miss G. That's all I know. Can you tell me anything about her? I had a special liking for her. In fact, I had a serious attraction to this woman. I thought to myself that if I ever got tied down, she would be the one."

Miss Caroline gazed into Nevada's eyes. Miss Caroline knew Miss G, as she was called, but how much information to share with this cowboy was another question.

Miss Caroline asked, "What is your name again, and just how sincere and serious are you about this woman? What makes you think she would be the one?"

"Well," Nevada replied. "I had been with her on and off for two years. I thought she felt the same for me, as I feel for her. I really do not know what happened, Miss Caroline. The last night I was with her, she made an about-face. Said she never wanted to see me again. She said she had taken up with another man from Kansas City, and that was that! No explanation! Then the gunslinger from Kansas City threatened to kill me if I ever see her again. The whole thing puzzles me, Miss Caroline. I thought she was in love with me. I figured when I came into town I'd try to look her up and get a satisfactory answer for myself."

"Mr. Granger," Miss Caroline asked. "How long are you going to be in town?"

"Several days, why?" he replied.

"Well, if you can come back here tomorrow night," Miss Caroline explained. "I'll have some information to share with you. That is, If Miss Gentry is willing to talk to you."

"So, that's her name?"

"Yes," Miss Caroline answered. "Miss Maggie Gentry. We all called her Miss G."

"Great!" Nevada exclaimed.

He then stood up, shook Miss Caroline's hand, and walked toward the door.

Then Miss Caroline said, "I can tell you one thing…no matter what the outcome is, she was very much in love with you, as you would say, but I can't even anticipate what the outcome will be."

As Nevada returned to the main floor of the saloon, he was very happy and somewhat relieved but puzzled because he flat did not know what happened between them or why it happened. Nevada noticed Josh was hooping and a'hollering, very drunk, but he did have a pile of money in his stack.

As Nevada walked over to Josh, he exclaimed, "Looks like you hit the jackpot!"

Josh quickly answered, "Just beginner's luck. I just hope it keeps growing and growing!"

Then Josh looked at his cards and said, "I'll call!"

When all the men laid down their cards, Josh had won again. Everybody was a hollering and a hooping and clapping.

One man stood up and bellowed out, "Another round of drinks on me."

Josh put his arm around the man, they toasted each other, and Josh remarked, "It's going to be a good night!"

Rex and Sherwin were at another table, staring at Josh.

Rex smiled. "Hope the whiskey does not get the best of him."

"Looks like he's doing pretty good," Sherwin observed. "But I know luck can change."

"Yeah," Rex added. "Couple of poor bets, and you could end up flat broken. Think we better check on Josh?"

"Probably so," Sherwin agreed. "Why don't you round up the boys, and we will head back to Miss Mabel's?"

Rex added, "We need to be up bright and early to check on the horses. You know we've got 700 miles to go before we get to Colorado Springs."

"Rex," Sherwin suggested. "Why don't you check on Roddy? Tell him we are leaving."

Sherwin headed up the stairs, and a young lady met him halfway. He relayed the message to her, and she went on upstairs to give the message to Roddy. Joining Sherwin and Nevada, Rex motioned to Josh that it was time to go.

"Oh, man!" he fussed.

But he knew Rex meant business, so he turned in his cards and joined the group. The men left the saloon.

While walking toward the stable, they heard Roddy hollering, "Wait, wait up!"

The next morning the men were all seated around the kitchen table. Miss Mabel and Abby were bringing the breakfast platters in and placing them on the table. Sausage, biscuits, hashbrowns, and eggs were on the menu. After Rex said Grace the men began to pass the dishes around.

"Did you fellas enjoy yourself last night?" Buck asked.

Josh spoke up first. "Well, if you call bringing in over three hundred dollars on the first night at The Blue Dog enjoying ourselves, then yes, I did enjoy myself."

Sherwin spoke up next. "Good you quit when you did. Always better to have a little pile of money rather than to go home empty-handed."

Then Rex spoke directly to Nevada. "Did you find anything out about that little gal you was courting last year?"

"Not yet," he responded. "Miss Caroline promised to give me some information tonight. I'm still puzzled about the whole situation."

"Pass the biscuits!" Josh hollered across the table.

"Watch your manners, boy," Buck reprimanded.

Miss Mabel heard the discussion from the other room, and she walked in with another platter of biscuits and sausage.

"Eat up, boys," Miss Mabel said. "We have plenty."

Then Mabel called to Abby. "We need more coffee."

Abby returned to the room with coffee and orange juice.

"Boys, we've got a lot to do today," said Rex. "Eat up and let's go get started."

One by one, the men got up, excused themselves, and began their chores for the day.

Then Rex turned to Buck and said, "Let's you and me

drive into town and get the supplies for the rest of the trip. I've kept a running list of needed supplies, and it shouldn't take long. "Saddle up," Buck responded, "I'll get the wagon, and we'll go into town."

As the men were leaving the corral, Roddy and Nevada were heading toward the stable, near the east side of the boardinghouse.

Roddy said, "I hope Gus is finished with the horses."

"Yes," Nevada responded. "Several of the horses need re-shoeing, and we certainly do not want any delays before we pick up the Appaloosas."

"When do you figure we'll get to Colorado Springs?" Rex asked.

"Probably by the end of the month," Nevada answered.

"The horses are coming from a territory north of Cheyenne up in the Dakotas," Sherwin added.

Nevada explained, "Several Indian traders are making the transaction."

"I hope we don't have any trouble," Roddy said.

"Me, too," Nevada added.

"Anything can happen when you deal with the Sioux Indians."

"Yes," Nevada said, then recollected, "I remember several years ago we had a three-week delay because of private negotiations."

"Yes, Rex was afraid we were going home empty-handed," Roddy added. "Oh, well, hope everything will go off as planned." Roddy tried to reassure himself.

Then Mr. Gus came out of the stable. "All the horses have been checked and re-shoed. Doctor Swearinger checked each horse, and you're ready to go."

Mr. Gus proudly said, "Great!"

Gus and Nevada shook hands. "We always appreciate the good work that you do." Nevada declared.

"We'll tell Rex we are ready to roll," Roddy said.

Then Roddy and Nevada went into the stable to see for themselves how the horses looked. After checking the horses and their hooves, Roddy and Nevada agreed everything looked good. When Rex and Buck reached Jefferson City, they headed right for the general store.

"Rex," Buck said. "You take care of the staple supplies, and I will get the traveling items."

Then Buck said, "Here, I've got a list for you. I've been keeping it since we went through The Wilderness Trail."

Tearing off the tail end of the list, Rex began looking through the store for the items on the list. Buck had several large boxes, each crammed full of different foods, needed for the next two months. As they went up and down the rows, he added a few items that were not on the list. Meanwhile, new blankets, kerosene oil lamps, and large canteens of water were added to the list of items needed. One of the men needed some new saddle equipment. His stirrups had gotten caught in some thick brush and barbed wire, and they tore apart. They were probably old to begin with. Regardless, these are items that have to be purchased to continue the journey.

After about an hour or so the men met back together, and Rex paid the storekeeper. The storekeeper thanked them and wished them a successful trip on to Colorado Springs. The boys left the store and headed back to Miss Mabel's boardinghouse.

As they were riding back, Rex said, "Hopefully, the

horses will be ready, and the Staunton Cowboys will be on their way."

"Right," Buck agreed. "Gus is good, and I'm sure he has completed his job."

When they reached Miss Mabel's, Sherwin met them at the gate. "I've squared everything with Miss Mabel, and, Rex, we are ready to go."

"Great!" Sherwin added. "Men, get word to the other boys, and we will be on our way."

The Staunton Cowboys were heading northeast towards Cheyenne. They made their last goodbyes and thank yous, and their journey continued. As they drove through Jefferson City, the boys longed to stop in for one last drink at The Blue Dog.

"No," Rex commanded. "We simply do not have the time."

Then Nevada rode up really close to Rex and whispered something to him.

"Okay," Rex said. "But you'd best catch up with us by dark."

Then Rex reminded him, "We're going by Cotton Springs."

"I remember," Nevada assured him. "Are you still dealing with Mr. Keith and Mr. Marvin?"

"Yes," Rex declared. "They'll meet us at the trading Ranch and will make our transaction."

"I'm good." Nevada turned his horse around back toward Jefferson City.

All the men knew where he was going. He was going back to the Blue Dog Saloon to get the information about Miss G. As he pushed open the saloon doors at The Blue

Dog, everything seemed quite slow. A couple of cowboys were at the card table. Several men were lined up at the bar, and the bartender was polishing the silver jigger glasses. Yes, everything seemed pretty slow compared to the action-packed saloon from last night. There were no ladies in sight.

Nevada went up to the bartender and asked for a drink. Then he told the bartender, "I'm Nevada Granger. I talked with Miss Caroline last night. She asked me to come in today. I need to see her about something."

"She's not in right now," the bartender noted. "Why don't you pick out a table? She'll be back shortly, I'm sure."

Well, Nevada knew Rex was a stickler for following his directions. But he did as the bartender asked. He went over to a table close to the door leading to Miss Caroline's office and took a seat at the table. An hour went by, then another hour went by. The saloon had picked up. Several more cowboys came in, some asking for drinks and some just strolling around the saloon. Nevada made his way back to the bar and asked the bartender, "Are you sure she's coming back today?"

"Yes, she said she'd be back around 1 p.m." Nevada looked at the clock. It was 2:30 p.m. So, he went back and sat down.

Another thirty minutes went by. Then, all at once, there was a tap on his shoulder. He looked around. It was Miss Caroline. She motioned for him to be quiet, and she directed him to her office. When he stepped inside of Miss Caroline's office, there was Miss G seated in a chair, and she had a baby in her arms.

He was quite surprised and shocked. Nevada looked

somewhat embarrassed. He was very glad to see Miss G. Nevada went over to the lady, seated on the chair. He gazed down into her green eyes, and looked at the baby.

Before he could say anything, Miss Caroline said, "Maggie, let me take the boy."

Miss Caroline and the baby boy left the room, leaving Nevada and Miss G all alone. Nevada lifted Miss G out of the chair, and, looking into her eyes, he stated again, "I love you. I do not know what all has happened, but my love for you is still stronger than ever."

Gazing back into his eyes, with tears streaming down her cheeks, she told him, "I've always loved you." Then, looking into his eyes, she said, "The boy is yours."

"What?" Nevada questioned. "Are you sure?"

"Yes, Nevada, the little boy is yours. Can't you tell? He is a spitting image of you," she explained.

"I'm not asking for anything," Miss G said. "I'm glad you know you have a son."

Nevada went over to the other chair next to the kerosene oil lamp and sat down.

"I don't understand." Nevada was puzzled.

Then Miss G tried to explain. "The Kansas City gunslinger knew I had a baby boy, and he knew the boy was yours. He threatened to kill you if you ever got involved with me again, so I pretended I didn't want to have anything to do with you."

Then Nevada asked her, "Do you love me?"

She answered, "Yes, but there's nothing we can do."

"What do you mean?" Nevada questioned her.

"Jim, my husband, has made an about-face with his life. He has become a respectable man, and we own a small ranch outside of town. He is raising the boy as our son, so you can see there's nothing we can do. It's too late."

Nevada seems stunned, "I do not know what to say."

"Neither do I," Miss G explained. "Except this is the end. I will never see you again, but I'll always love you."

Nevada stood up, embraced Miss G, and said, "Goodbye, Maggie. Take care of my boy."

"I will, Nevada, I will," Maggie replied. "I promise you with my life, I will take care of your son."

"What's his name?" Nevada asked.

"We call him Nevada."

With tears streaming down his face, Nevada left the saloon and returned to the trail ride. The cowboys knew when they left Jefferson City they were heading toward Colorado Springs. The last trail ride was very dangerous, when the men had to travel through the Nebraska territory. Everything had gone as planned. However, the Cowboys were very tired. They had lost a lot of sleep. The whirling sandy winds had caused the delay, as they travel through the Great Plains. Looking toward the west, you could see the great Rocky Mountains. The men were always excited as the mountain range begin to appear. This meant that the journey was almost halfway completed. Just pick up the Appaloosas and head back to Staunton, West Virginia.

Rex explained the situation. "We are supposed to meet the McKinley brothers due south of Cheyenne, near Colorado Springs. The McKinleys have a big spread, a trading ranch. Carlton has been dealing with these men for years."

"Has he always been pleased with their business?" Josh asked.

"Yes," Buck responded. "The brothers are fair, and the

Appaloosas are top stock."

"I do not believe..." Rex added. "...that Mr. Carlton would not agree to deal with anyone else on this matter. Carlton usually wires the money several months in advance, and the ponies are selected according to the breed."

"We usually try to purchase a hundred head each year," Sherwin added. "Carlton has already got most of the ponies sold. Several farms out east specialize in Appaloosas, and they depend on Mr. Staunton to bring the ponies from Cheyenne."

"Couldn't be better," Josh added.

"I can't say for sure," Sherwin interrupted.

"I'm sure," Rex announced. "Go on back to the trail riders and tell them we will bed down for tonight and get to Cheyenne sometime tomorrow evening,"

Arriving at the foot of the Rocky Mountains, you could see the towering mountains in the background. Marvin and his brother, Keith, had a rolling homestead. Two large homes, several large barns, and a water irrigation system had been built and constructed to hold water from the North Platte River. Even when it was the dry season, the McKinley brothers always had enough water to meet the demands of their animals. As the Staunton Cowboys made their way to the Bar M Ranch, the McKinley brothers were standing near the first fenced-in area. As the men got closer Keith made the first gesture to meet the trail riders. Barton followed.

"Good afternoon," Keith McKinley greeted the Cowboys. "We were expecting you all last week."

"That sandstorm delayed us. The winds were so bad, we

had to bed down." Nevada explained. "The horses couldn't see, and we knew if they got frightened, they would stampede. So, we thought it was best to stop until the winds cleared up."

Rex and Sherwin got off the horses, walked toward the brothers and shook hands.

"How are you all?" Keith asked. "And how is everything back east?"

"Well," Rex began. "You know all about the flooding."

"Yes," Marvin added. "We heard it was really bad."

"Yeah," Sherwin spoke up. "Carlton had to close down Staunton. Most of the people went to Charlottesville to stay until the floodwaters receded."

"Is everything going to be all right?" Keith asked.

"We certainly hope so," Rex replied. "We got a lot of folks depending on Staunton Plantation."

As the men walked toward the second fenced in area, Keith said, "See the red markers? We have selected those ponies for you all. They are nice and ready to go."

"How many mares? How many studs?"

After looking the ponies over, Rex and Sherwin were satisfied with their purchase.

Then Keith remarked, "You all come on in and rest up. Granny has the dinner waiting. She had a sneaky feeling you cowboys just might come rolling in here sometime today, and she was right."

Keith walked on toward the big house, and Marvin stayed behind giving directions to the

cowboys on where they were to bunk down. They were instructed to put their horses in the regular stable on the property at the usual place.

"Yes," Marvin replied. "Barton is still taking care of your horses. He'll show you where to bunk down, and he'll take care of your horses. Then you men come on to the house. Granny is waiting."

As the men came through the front door, Granny was the first to greet them. "Been worried about you boys! We were looking for you all for the last two weeks. Figured there had been some trouble somewhere on the ride."

"You are right, Granny," Sherwin explained. "Sand storms delayed us about a week and a half."

"Come on in," Granny suggested. "Usually, I suggest you boys wash up first, but I understand completely. Just wash your hands and come on in to the table. Dinner is waiting for you all."

The men gathered around the kitchen table. Marvin said grace, and the men began to enjoy the delicious food which is been prepared for them. After eating and resting for the night, they bid farewell to the McKinley family. The Staunton Cowboys started the remainder of the trail ride back to Staunton with the hundred head of Appaloosas. The first half of the journey was complete. The first part of the trail ride was the easy part. Picking up the Appaloosas and herding them back was the hard part. There were three major obstacles.

First of all, the route back to Staunton, West Virginia, had to follow a safe trail back. Mountain ranges, gullies, rivers, and streams could present hazardous problems. Careful planning and cautionary measures had to be thought out before the trail riders start back home. Then the weather was always a major consideration. Sandstorms, dust storms, twisters, unpredicted hailstorms, and heavy rains could always cause problems in getting the Appaloosas back to Staunton Plantation. But the last obstacle, and perhaps the most crucial, was to protect the herd. Outlaws roamed the territory and were willing to kill in order to steal your ponies. The trail riders had to be very focused returning home. Scouts had to travel miles ahead to search out any signs of possible danger. Just over the next hill or around the next bend or at the end of a river stream, outlaws, thieves and possible Indian warriors could be planning their next move.

The Staunton boys had to be ready to defend themselves and the herd. The cowboys were about fifty miles out of Colorado Springs. Rex and Sherwin were riding together. Rex addressed Sherwin and said, "I know Carlton is going to be awfully mad."

"I figured he would be," Sherwin responded. "He bargained for a hundred head, and the McKinley brothers came up lacking. Wonder what happened…"

Rex then responded, "Keith promised the other ten would come in the cattle drive next month."

Looking around, another cowboy from the trail drive was riding up really fast. It was Roddy, and he was excited.

He hollered, "Trouble in the east flank!"

Rex looked at Sherwin. "Can you handle it? Ride ahead and halt the others."

Then Roddy and Sherwin rode toward the back of the herd, and Rex rode ahead to inform the others. The herd was passing through the old Mormon and Oregon Trail near Chimney Rock. Not being familiar with the territory several ponies strayed away from the herd and got tangled up in some barbed wire belonging to Mister Daniel

Freeman. Mr. Freeman was very cooperative, and he told Sherwin and Roddy just how to get out the barbed wire.

Then Mr. Freeman admitted, "I knew there was a herd of ponies coming through. I just didn't have a chance to warn you all before you got here."

Sherwin broke in and asked, "How many ponies strayed?"

"Terrence, my boy, said three or four. He could not get them out of the barbed wire because the gully had eroded so deep."

"Son," Mr. Freeman suggested. "It's late. Why don't you all go out to the south pasture and take a look for yourself. You all can plan to get them out first thing after the sun comes up, Terrence, my son, will show you the way." Then he inquired, "Who is the trail boss?"

"Rex Rogers from Staunton plantation," Sherwin answered.

Mr. Freeman then asked, "Who are the cowboys? West Virginia trail riders?"

Roddy answered, "Yes."

"Mr. Staunton is a good man. I'll wire him that you all will be detained a day or two. Don't want to chance losing those thoroughbreds."

Mr. Freeman then told his son to lead Sherwin and Roddy toward the South pasture. Toward the backside there was a steep gully and several rolls of old barbed wire which had been thrown in the gully.

Terrence peered into the dark gully and shined his lantern that way and said, "The horses must have gotten scared and stampeded right through the new fence that surrounded the eroded gully."

As they stood with the kerosene lanterns, the men could see that they could not do anything before daybreak. Sherwin turned toward Terrence. "Tell your Pa that I am pretty sure we'll bed down on his property and get the ponies out tomorrow."

As the two trail riders, Sherwin and Roddy, were riding off, Mr. Freeman came out toward them and said, "Tell your trail boss to come on in bright and early for fresh coffee and biscuits. My daughter is the best cook in Nahnatchka."

Both the trail riders looked puzzled by the strange name and said, "Huh?"

Then Mister Freeman explained, "Nahnatchka is an old Indian word that means flat water. That's what the Omahas called the Platte River. Early settlers said the stream was a mile wide and an inch deep, always muddy and it flowed upside down."

Sherwin then remarked, "Sounds great. Sun up, we'll be here."

Then the two cowboys rode off.

To continue the trail ride on toward Staunton with Appaloosas, the men were very glad to get the situation cleared up. The ponies that were tangled up in the barbed wire were freed. The ponies were scratched up and bruised, but no major tragedies. The breakfast at Mr. Freeman's was greatly appreciated, and the trail riders were glad to get back on their journey. Rex and Sherwin had discussed the matter of the journey in great detail. Since the floodwaters had to recede, Carlton had sent the Cowboys two months ahead of the regular schedule. The house workers had been sent to Charlottesville.

A few people stayed on at Staunton, but most were sent

on because there was nothing to do until the floodwaters went down. The Cowboys had never started two months early, so they did not know what to anticipate. Weather complications are of major concern. Thick snow was on the ground. The sky was a bright reflection on the snow on the ground. The sky lit up in anger as the swirling winds circled the plains. Keeping the herd together and keeping them calm was a tumultuous task. Each cowboy was stationed in a certain area to keep Appaloosas together.

Riding along, Nevada spoke up. "We ought to arrive in Wichita within a few days."

"Yeah," Roddy said, reminding him, "But you remember last year. Those ranchers were pretty upset when we crossed their territory."

Nevada began to remember. "But we didn't have any idea that the land survey had changed hands, and we just figured the route would be the same."

"We'd better check with Rex," Roddy suggested. "I'd hate to run into that same situation again. I'll ride on ahead and see what he says."

So, Roddy rode on, leaving Nevada with about a third of the ponies. Buck and Josh were at the end of the trail ride. They were driving the wagon with about a third of the ponies. The sun was going down in the western sky. You could see Woodland's Bluff in the distance. The bluff was a narrow entrance between two mountain ranges. The bluff was about a thirty-mile stretch up the mountain and down the other side. But the downward side was a dangerous slope, so the ponies had to be very careful and not get frightened. Rex had circled around to get the ponies in line to begin the journey through the bluff.

Sherwin and Rex knew they had to hasten along to make the thirty miles before dark. All had gone well. The horses traveled very calmly through the bluff and were almost down the dangerous slope, when all of a sudden, the horses began to panic and stampede down the slope. Several ponies fell, but luckily, they were not injured. The Cowboys got them under control, and the ponies were able to rejoin the herd. From out of the darkness, four rustlers appeared and began to take over the herd.

"Lordy, Lordy," Roddy prayed. "What do I do now?"

No guns were fired. The men apparently were professional rustlers because, like clockwork, the rustlers took over the herd. Nevada was left standing at the foot of the mountain. Roddy returned dumbfounded. The next morning Nevada and Roddy had to resume the journey without the ponies.

The men headed out toward Wichita to catch up with the rest of the trail riders. When they got to the outskirts of Wichita, they were very much shocked. The stolen herd of thirty Appaloosas were all outside roped together. As they rode up toward the Appaloosa herd, Sherwin met the two men.

Roddy exclaimed, "What in the hell is going on?"

The cowboys simply did not understand what had transpired.

Then Rex began to explain the situation. "The Apache Tribe had planned on attacking us and stealing the entire herd. Chi Howie got wind of this and notified his Comanche friends. They planned a counterattack. The Comanches rounded up the ponies and brought them to us in Wichita."

"Come on in, boys," Buck suggested.

Then Sherwin advised the cowboys, "You all need to rest. I know it's been a very upsetting night. You really need to rest before we continue the trail ride."

"Yes," Nevada exclaimed. "Don't ever leave me alone with the responsibility on my shoulders to do anything like this again! Hell, I could have had a stroke. I'm not up to this shit."

At that the men rode on into Wichita to spend the night, and the next day they continued their trail ride.

It was February at Staunton Plantation. Jessica Leigh, Rosie, Samantha, Cotton, and Rooster have handled the work around the plantation reasonably well. As you recall, the rest of the Staunton Plantation workers were sent to Charlottesville to work while the floodwaters receded. Looking over the plantation the ground was still wet, but there was no standing water visible. At the breakfast table, Carlton is enjoying his daily breakfast.

"Things are looking up, Jessica Leigh, things are looking up," Carlton reassured her. "I feel sure you'll be able to return to school in the fall. Perhaps you'll even be able to attend the summer session."

"Are you sure, Papa?" Jessica questioned him. "Are you sure?"

"Well," he added. "I do believe by spring the grounds will be dry enough to do the new planting. The boys will be returning with Appaloosas and hopefully everything can get back to normal."

With a big sigh of relief, Jessica Leigh got out of her chair, walked over to her dad, and, putting her arms around him, she said, "I'm so proud of you. This has been a very stressful situation, and you have handled it well. Do you believe you'll be able to hire everybody back to work here at Staunton?"

"I certainly hope so," he responded. "Teddy and I riding over to Charlottesville in a few days to check on everything. Hopefully we will be able to start bringing everybody back by the end of next month."

"Through with your breakfast, Mr. Carlton?" Rosie asked.

"Yes." Carlton nodded. "And, I might add, you have done an excellent job of replacing Miss Cadelia while she has been recuperating in Charlottesville."

"How is she doing?" Rosie asked.

"The doctor says she's coming along fine. However, don't relax too much. I do not know if she'll ever be able to do all the things she did before the heart attack," Carlton cautioned her.

"Teddy reassures me that she is doing much better, but the stress of running the Staunton household may be too much for her."

"It's too much for me, sir, it's too much for me, too," Rosie admitted.

"Don't be so modest, Rosie, you've done a remarkable job." Carlton tried to reassure her.

"You sure have, Rosie," Jessica Leigh added. "I do believe you could actually replace Miss Cadelia – if need be, of course."

Carlton then interrupted. "Don't worry yourself anymore, Rosie. When the time comes, you will be able to replace Miss Cadelia with confidence."

Jessica hugged Rosie and agreed, "You'll do fine! Just

fine!"

The next day, Carlton and Teddy are on horseback. They are riding the east side of the property.

"Things are looking good," Teddy exclaimed.

"I'll say," Carlton admitted. "Things are looking good. I'm surprised that the ground has dried so fast."

Carlton and Teddy stopped the horses, got off, and began to run their hands and fingers through the new grass and brush.

"I think we can begin planning any time now," Carlton acknowledged.

"I think so," Teddy agreed.

"How does the Westside appear?" Teddy asked.

"About the same," Carlton answered. "I think I'll cut the east field and double up in the west. I feel sure everything will be okay, but for this first year we'll need to be careful and very cautious. I don't want to plant more than we can handle."

They got back on their horses. Teddy then asked, "What are you going to do about Jessica's schooling?"

"Well," Carlton told him. "I know she is anxious to get back. That young man she has been courting has wired her several times, inquiring when she is returning to Wilshire."

"And just who is this young man, and is she serious about him?" Teddy asked.

"She met him at the Fall Festival," Carlton explained. "It was a get acquainted dance hosted by the West Virginia University in Morgantown, West Virginia. I think they both had a good time. His family is in the oil business, and he is from Texas. But then the floods came, and you know the rest."

Teddy remembered, "Yes, you had to go to the Academy and bring her home."

"I do hope I can take her back this summer to enroll in the summer session," Carlton declared. "I figure about mid-summer. Staunton Plantation will be up and running, and I am glad. This has been a tiresome ordeal, and everybody will be glad when things are back to normal."

Then Teddy broke in. "We'd better be getting back. I'm sure Rosie has dinner ready for us, and I'm hungry!" The two men rode on back to Staunton plantation, where the rest of the group met them for dinner.

By the end of April, all the workers sent to Charlottesville while the floodwaters receded were back at Staunton Plantation. Everything was back to normal except Miss Cadelia was in no physical condition to do the domestic chores to run the household. Rosie had been moved from the Negro quarters to the main house. Rosie and Miss Cadelia were now sharing a room. Miss Cadelia's room was located next to the kitchen, and it was a large room so both ladies could use the bedroom.

Meanwhile, back in the Negro cabins, the workers were elated about their return home to Staunton.

"I sho' am glad to be home again," Leddy Gail breathed another sigh of relief. "It has been a long year."

"Don't fool yourself, Leddy Gail," Cotton added. "It's been rough on all of us who stayed here."

"Yeah," Rooster piped in. "Me and Cotton had to do everything on this here farm, and I do mean everything there was to do."

"I'm not going to fuss with you, Cotton. I just know I'm glad to be home," Leddy Gail remarked again.

Then Rooster spoke up. "So, Leddy Gail, how is Miss Cadelia?"

"Well," Leddy Gail declared. "She is alive, but putting that baby skull back in the grandfather clock did her in. Doctor Teddy says she can't walk. Her heart can't take the stress of physical activity."

"So, what's going to happen to her?" Cotton quizzed.

"Well, I do believe Miss Cadelia will be doing a lot of sitting and directing from her wheelchair," Samantha added. "And she can do that."

"She sure can," Helsinki agreed.

Samantha then announced, "Jessica Leigh said Miss Cadelia will keep her room in the big house, and Rosie's bed will be moved in there with Miss Cadelia. The two of them get along very well. Rosie has been assisting Miss Cadelia for a long time, so Jessica Leigh said it will all work out fine."

"It sounds like Mr. Carlton has pretty much figured out the situation." Cotton muttered. "Yes," Samantha replied, "and I hope it works! We will all be in terrible shape if Miss Cadelia is not around." Then Samantha informed the group, "Jessica Leigh will be going back to Wilshire Academy for the summer session. I sure am going to miss her." "We all will miss her," Cotton added, "she has been a big help this past year, and I know her dad will hate to see her leave."

CHAPTER 13

Staunton's Wedding

Two years had passed at Staunton Plantation. Excitement was in the air. Jessica Leigh had just graduated from Wilshire Academy in the east. When she returned to the Academy, she and Anthony both completed their studies. Very romantically involved, they knew they would be wed. The Staunton household had been very busy preparing for the wedding celebration. Up on the second floor in Jessica Leigh's bedroom, Jessica is trying on her gown for its final fitting. Two French designers, Monsieur Louie and Monsieur Lateen, are busy babbling in French about the last and final adjustments that need to be made. Isabella Brantley and Hortense are beaming with excitement. Several of Anthony's fraternity brothers are here for the wedding. The young men had been asked to be groomsmen. There were several festivities plan prior to the wedding, and Isabella and Hortense were very happy to enjoy time with these young men.

"Hurry, Jessica!" Isabella exclaimed. "The picnic is going on now! The horse races are so much fun," Hortense bragged. "And Alex is so attentive to me."

"I'm glad you like him. He is a very likable person once

you get to know him," Jessica explained.

"We're going on back to the festivities," Isabella remarked. "Charles and Alex are waiting on us."

"I'll be down once Monsieur Louie and Monsieur Lateen finish my dress."

"Girls," Jessica Leigh told them. "Daddy has planned a sunset dance at the Pavilion. Be sure you all plan to attend. All of the Staunton residents and the town people will be there. Daddy has planned a magnificent affair. I know will all enjoy it."

"Great!" Hortense exclaimed. "I can wear my pink organza." She smiled as she thought to herself, I'm sure Alex will think I'm pretty!

The girls went on down to the afternoon activities.

The long picnic tables ran the length of the front of the home. White lace tablecloths and imported linens decorated the tables. Miss Cadelia was seated in her wheelchair, looking her finest. And as usual, she was quite busy giving her instructions to the domestic help. Rosie and Samantha were grumbling to themselves.

Rosie complained, "Fast as I could do one task, she tells me what went wrong."

Samantha agreed, "Meats go all one side and desserts go on the other side, but she's had me change the platter several times. She says she wants the table to be perfect."

"Perfect, my ass!" Rosie hollered back. "She is too old to be in charge of this affair."

"I agree," Samantha stated.

Cotton, Rooster, Helsinki, Sylvester, Rosetta, and the cowboys had been moving chairs and benches in for the picnic. The whole front fawn looked like a picnic on the grounds affair, held at church socials.

Aunt Martha looked her best. Uncle Josh had died, and she and Doctor McKinley had married. Doctor McKinley persuaded Aunt Martha to come to Wilshire to teach, and, needless to say, they finally married. They both stayed on at Wilshire Academy. However, they both were invited guests to Staunton Plantation for the magnificent wedding.

By the end of the week, the wedding took place. The weather was beautiful. The chairs and benches from the picnic were all turned toward the plantation home. Greenery ran from one end of the front porch to the other. Fresh roses were intertwined in between all the greenery. Leslie Tatum and her father, Edgar, were also invited guests. I do think Leslie secretly hoped she could entice Carlton enough that he would ask her to stay on a while, thus giving her another opportunity to possibly stir up a romance. And yes, Leslie Charlene was ravishing beautiful.

Sally Mae Ashwood stayed on in Staunton, and she lucked out. Uncle Teddy hired her as his receptionist, and I did believe wedding bells would in the air for those two. Sabrina, George, and Agnes were simply delighted. Sally Mae had moved up in society when she went out to Chicago, and when she returned to Staunton her upper-class status rubbed off on all of them. Even poor old Georgie was standing up proud and respected. He was a changed young man.

As the music began, Carlton escorted his daughter up the front steps to the plantation home. They were met with Anthony Lucas and his father. The priest then had the young people recite their wedding vows, and they are locked together in matrimony.

CHAPTER 14

Indian Hopes Fulfilled

One year had passed. White Feather had a trading post outside Calhoun City. Indians from surrounding communities were congregated inside the cabin. All the Indians were well aware that the baby that Jessica Leigh was carrying was about to be born, and this special child would be their savior in helping the Red Man acquire the lands that white men had stolen from them decades before. Hearing about the baby's birth, the Red Men knew that M. Shay and her spiritual insights would save the Red Man in America.

ABOUT THE AUTHOR

MARGARET JOANNE RICE is a retired educator. She holds a Master's Degree from Mississippi State University. She has taught elementary school and served as a guidance counselor at the Middle and High School levels. The author has always had a desire to write and has dabbled with the desire for years. It was hard to write before retirement because of obligations to family and work. Those years raising three children hindered the writing process. Ten years ago, the writer was forced to retire because of a kidney transplant. The children were grown and, suddenly, she had time to write.

J. Kenkade
PUBLISHING®

Our Motto
"Transforming Life Stories"

Publish Your Book With Us

Our All-Inclusive Publishing Package
Professional Proofreading & Editing
Interior Design & Cover Design
Manuscript Writing Assistance
Ghostwriting & More

For Manuscript Submission or other inquiries:
www.jkenkadepublishing.com
(501) 482-JKEN

Also Available from
J. Kenkade Publishing

ISBN: 978-1-944486-20-4
Purchase at www.jkenkadepublishing.com

As a school counselor and mother, the author became extremely
concerned about her ovarian cancer diagnosis, nutrition, and
weight loss. Research shows that people do not get second
opinions about their health, although health professionals do
not see second opinions as a breach of trust from people. This
book is a personal guide on how to handle any illness that a
man or woman may face in life. This personal cancer story will
make you laugh, cry, but overall, will empower you by faith.
Join Debra in her journey of survival in "Bound by Faith".

Also Available from
J. Kenkade Publishing

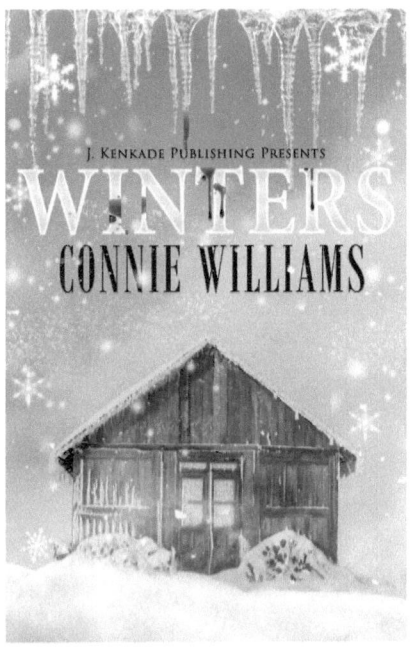

ISBN: 978-1-944486-40-2
Purchase at www.jkenkadepublishing.com

Winters is a captivating and passionate Christian suspense novel about a powerful, spiritual black family who is anointed and ordained by God Almighty. You will feel love, pain, heartaches, compassion, grace, mercy, suffering, and God's spirit, all in one story. Find out why Winters is about the coldest season of the year in more ways than one. Come and live in the minds and hearts of Stella, Abe, Mr. Perkins, The Langley family, Hattie, Benjamin, and Minnie. So much more awaits you in this powerful Christian suspense novel. Both fiction and nonfiction, Winters will give you a chill like never before!

Also Available from J. Kenkade Publishing

ISBN: 978-1-944486-19-8

Purchase at www.jkenkadepublishing.com

Life shouldn't be happening to us: we should be happening to life. This is what living in excellence is all about: Using every talent, gift, capacity and revelation that God has equipped us with and reaching our fullest potential. In this 31-Day guide, you will discover how meditating and reflecting on the word of God can pull you into His divine plan for your life. Prepare to expand past mediocrity and live a life of excellence.

www.ingramcontent.com/pod-product-compliance
Lightning Source LLC
Chambersburg PA
CBHW020748250626
47155CB00003B/971